"Robin McKinley paints a magical landscape that will delight and enchant hearts young and old."

—Joan D. Vinge

"THE DOOR IN THE HEDGE opens onto a world of magic that is both muscular and enchanting. Robin McKinley obviously loves the music of the old tales, but she adds melodies all her own, and that is what makes these stories so very very special and so very very unforgettable."

—Jane Yolen

"McKinley, in these stories, is afraid neither of great beauty nor of great evil. She has the gift of taking these stories and retelling them with love. . . . "

—*Science Fiction Review*

" . . . adds subtlety, complexity, and suspense to what is only tersely stated in Grimm. Like a musical theme and variations the telling is full of digressions and decorations—arpeggios of ideas and language—that add new depth to an old tale."

—*Horn Book*

"This collection should interest readers of all ages who never tire of wizards and fairyland."

—*Washington Post*

The DOOR in the HEDGE

ROBIN McKINLEY

ACE FANTASY BOOKS
NEW YORK

THE DOOR IN THE HEDGE

An Ace Fantasy Book / published by arrangement with
William Morrow and Company, Inc.

PRINTING HISTORY
First Ace printing / July 1982
Second printing / December 1984

ISBN: 0-441-15314-3

Ace Fantasy Books are published by The Berkley Publishing Group,
200 Madison Avenue, New York, New York 10016.
PRINTED IN THE UNITED STATES OF AMERICA

CONTENTS

The
Stolen
Princess

PROLOGUE

THE LAST mortal kingdom before the unmeasured sweep of Faerieland begins has at best held an uneasy truce with its unpredictable neighbor. There is nothing to show a boundary, at least on the mortal side of it; and if any ordinary human creature ever saw a faerie—or at any rate recognized one—it was never mentioned; but the existence of the boundary and of faeries beyond it is never in doubt either.

The people who live in those last lands are a little special themselves, and either they breed true or the children grow up and leave for less suspenseful countryside. Those who do leave are rarely heard from again, and then only in stiff or hasty letters written to assure friends and family of their well-being; they never return in person. But some of those who leave remember what they have left; and the memories are not all taken up with things that go bump in the night (which are never faeries, who know better than to make noise) or the feeling of being watched while standing at the center of a wide, sunny, sweet-smelling meadow and spinning helplessly in your tracks seeking for the shadow that is always behind you. For much of that watchfulness is friendly: if you lie down by the side of a brook and fall asleep, the murmuring water sends pleasant dreams of love and courage; and if a child loses its way in a forest, it finds its way out again before it is anything more than tired and scratched and cross and hungry.

And there are years when no babies at all are stolen from their cradles, and new mothers laugh, and grandparents gloat, and new fathers spin fabulous dreams of future greatness and trip over their own feet. But there are also years when expectant mothers go about with white faces and dread the arrival of what they most want, and the fathers listen anxiously for a child's first cry, but are not soothed when finally they hear it. And the father's first question, as is the way of fathers everywhere, is "A boy or a girl?" But his reasons, in this last country, are a little different. The faeries always choose boy babies.

The story is still told that once, perhaps a century ago, or perhaps two, a five-weeks girl was snatched away through a window her parents knew only too well that they had bolted carefully from the inside. But after two days—or rather, nights, for all immortal thievery occurs in the dark hours—the baby was returned.

There was never any question of a changeling. The whole silly idea of changelings was invented by lazy parents too far inland for any faintest whiff of faerie shores to have reached them; parents who cannot think of any other reason why their youngest, or middle, or eldest, or next-to-somethingest child should be so regrettable; they know they aren't to blame.

So there was no shadow in these parents' overjoyed

minds. But they were good people, and thoughtful, and after telling everyone they knew just once about the miraculous return, they never mentioned it again. Except once to the girl herself when she was almost grown; and she nodded, and looked thoughtful, but said nothing; and the uneasy dreams she had had for as long as she could remember, about impossible things that insisted that they were to be believed, stopped abruptly. She never mentioned the dreams to anyone either. Loose talk about faeries, dreams, and impossible things was not encouraged. It might be dangerous.

Six weeks after the little girl's marvelous adventure a family that lived only two streets over from her family lost its baby—a boy. He was the third child: he had two older sisters. He was not returned; nothing was ever heard of him again.

That was always the way of it. Nothing was ever again heard of the lost children; that was what, in the end, made it so terrible. The little girl who was returned seemed none the worse for wear; but then she had only been gone two days, and since she had been brought back she must have been a mistake. There was some thought, rarely mentioned aloud, that the fact that the faeries treated their mistakes kindly, or at least had been generous enough to bring this particular one back, was a good omen for the treatment of those they kept. It was this idea, persisting in the backs of people's minds, that made the retelling of the story of the baby that was returned so common. It was all the comfort they had. What happened to all the other ones, the ones that disappeared forever?

But the parents of girls are not to be envied either. A

boy, if he survives his first year, is safe. It is the girls who at last have the harder time of it, because it is when they reach their early blush of womanly beauty, between the ages, say, of sixteen and nineteen—it is then that they are in danger. And as it is the strong, handsome, happy boys that are taken, so it is the wisest and most beautiful girls—the girls who come home early from the parties they most enjoy, and leave their friends desolate behind them, because they know their parents are worrying at their being out so late; the same girls who never themselves think about being stolen because they have far too much else to do with their time and talents.

If a girl reaches twenty, she may breathe easier and think about marrying. But she has arrived safely at the cost of the cheerful carelessness of her youth; and it is too late for her to regain it now.

But the land was a good land, and its true people could not desert it, for they loved it; and it seemed that the land loved them in return; even if there were those who found the land's curious awareness of the people who stood or walked upon it disquieting. And sometimes even those who had been born and raised there left to find some country that would not keep them awake at night with its silence. Perhaps, bordering Faerieland, as it did, the touch of immortality made this land richer, more beautiful even than it might otherwise have been; and perhaps that touch lay gently on the people themselves. But for whatever reason, the land had been lived in for hundreds of years, and the people built their houses and barns and shops, and tilled their fields, and worked at their crafts, and married and . . . had children.

There was some commerce between them and less enchanted countries, and it was often observed that if you dared buy anything from that land, it lasted longer or tasted better or was more beautiful than its like from other origins; but the market for these things was limited because the commoner sort of mortal often found that things from that last land were a little hard to live with. They preyed on your mind; you had the feeling that they were breathing if you turned your back on them. Even a loaf of bread from that strange wheat could give you uncanny dreams—or insights into your neighbor all the more unnerving because they were accurate.

But its true people didn't care; and as some left it, others came, having tasted its wine, perhaps, or worn a cloak woven from its flax, and felt themselves somehow transformed, if only a little bit—just enough to make them restless, enough to make them come and see the strange living land themselves. And some of these looked long, and settled; and it, whatever it was, crept into the eyes of those who stayed, and into their blood, so they could not bear the thought of leaving, whatever dooms might hang over them if they remained.

There was something else, never discussed, and shunned even in the farthest secret reaches of the mind, but still present. No family was ever ended by the faeries' attentions. The first-born were rarely taken; usually they were the second- or third- or fourth-born. And never more than one child from a family disappeared, even if the entire family was spectacular in its beauty and charm and general desirability. This meant that the worst never quite happened; the spirit and will were never quite broken.

And in that uncommonly beautiful land, living under that particular sky, it was difficult if not impossible not to recover from almost anything but death itself.

But this narrow boon, this last hope not quite betrayed, was not talked about—not because of the simple dreadfulness of being grateful that only one child is forfeit. No, there was something else which cut even deeper: the omniscience indicated by the faeries' choice. First children were, in fact, sometimes taken, and how could the invisible thieves know in advance that more children would be born? Or that some sudden sickness would not take away the one or two that remained? But these things never happened; the faeries always knew. It wasn't something that those who had to live with it found themselves capable of thinking about. There were always the other things to think about, the good things.

Perhaps it came out even in the end; perhaps even a little better than even. The land was peaceful, and evidently always had been; even the history books could recount no wars. When there were storms at harvest time or sullen wet springs when the seeds died underground, somehow there was always just enough left to get everyone through the winter. And childless couples who desperately wanted children did eventually have one—or perhaps two; and if the faeries snatched one, they were still one better off than they had once feared they would remain. And so the years passed, and one generation gave way to the next, and the oldest trees in the oldest forests grew a little taller and a little thicker still; and the fireside tales of a family became the legends of a country.

But that same time that changed a quiet story into a

far-striding legend changed also the people who told and retold it. The world turned, and new stories rose up, and the legends of the old days faltered a little, or turned themselves in their course to keep up with the lives of their people, and the lives of great-grandchildren of those they had first known. Perhaps even the immortal ones beyond the borders of this last land felt the change in some fashion: for that they ventured at all, and for whatever reason, into mortal realms risked them to some sense of mortal lives and cares. Perhaps.

PART ONE

THE FAERIES had never been much noted for stealing members of the royal family of that last kingdom, perhaps because that family was more noted for its political acumen and a rather ponderous awareness of its own importance than for lightness of foot and spirit or beauty of face and form. But the current Queen's own sister, her twin sister, on the eve of their seventeenth birthday, had been stolen; and the Queen herself had never quite gotten over it. Or so everyone else thought: the Queen tried not to think of it at all.

The twins had been their royal parents' only children, and they were as beautiful as dawn, as spring, as your favorite poem and your first love: as beautiful as the rest of their family—aunts, uncles, cousins, and cousins-several-times-removed—were kind and stuffy and inclined to stoutness. The twins were kind, too, probably as kind as they were beautiful, which could not have been said of their worthy but plump parents.

Alora was the eldest by about half an hour, and so it was understood that she would eventually be Queen; but this cast no shadow between her and Ellian her sister, as you knew at once when you saw them together. And they were always together. Alora was fair and Ellian dark; it was easy to tell them apart with your eyes open. But with your eyes shut, it was impossible: they both had the same husky, slightly breathless voice, and they thought so much alike that you could expect the same comment from either of them. The people loved them; loved them so much that no one felt the desire to indulge in a preference for one sister over the other.

Not that they were stupidly interchangeable. They understood that the sympathy between them was so great that it left them quite free: and so Alora played the flute, and Ellian the harp; Ellian preferred horseback riding and Alora bathing in the lake, where she could outswim many of the fish, while Ellian paddled and floated and got her hair in her eyes and laughed. Alora could sing and Ellian could not. And each wore clothes that suited her individual coloring best; they made no mistakes here. But while they each rode a white mare on state occasions, Ellian's had fire in its eye and a curl to its lip, while Alora had to wear spurs to keep hers from falling asleep.

They slept in the same room, their tall canopied princesses' beds each pushed under a tall mullioned window. The room was large enough for both of them and their ladies-in-waiting and their royal robes not to get too severely in one another's way when they were dressing for a high court dinner, but not so large that they could not whisper to each other when they should have been asleep, and not lose the whispers into the high carved ceiling and the deep rugs and curtains. And so it was that when Alora opened her eyes on her seventeenth birthday and saw the sun shining as though he were convinced that this was the finest day he had ever seen and he must make the most of it, she looked across the room to her sister's bed and found it empty. She knew at once what had happened, although neither of them had ever thought of it before. If Ellian had gone out early, she would have awakened her sister first, in case she would like to accompany her—as Alora would have. They always accompanied each other. The little blue flowers called faeries'-eyes scattered across the coverlet were not more dreadful to her now than the fact of the empty bed itself.

A few minutes later when they found her, Alora was curled up on her sister's bed, weeping silently and hopelessly into her sister's pillow. When they lifted her up, they were surprised by a faint mysterious smell from the bruised flowers she had lain upon. The ladies bundled the coverlet up, flowers and all, and took it away, and burnt it.

The Queen and the ladies-in-waiting cried and wailed till the whole palace was infected, and the people who were gathered in the palace courtyard ready to cheer the opening festivities of the Princesses' birthday groaned aloud when they heard the news, given by the King himself with tears running down his face; and many wept as bitterly as Alora herself as they went their sorry ways homeward.

But while everyone else was sorry, they also at last shook themselves out of it and went on with their lives. Alora did not. She felt that she had only half a life left, and that a pale and quiet one. Her worried parents decided that perhaps the best thing to do for her was to marry her off quickly and let her begin housekeeping; it might also remind her of her responsibilities. She would be Queen someday, and her current listlessness would not do at all in a monarch. Her betrothed was willing—it was no state marriage of convenience for him: he had been desperately in love with her for three years, since she had first smiled at him, and was even unhappier than her parents that she smiled no more—and she was, well, she was fond of him and supposed she didn't mind. He was a cousin, but so many times removed that while he was indisputably kind, he was neither stout nor pompous; and in her weaker moments she thought he was quite handsome; and in her official moments she thought he would make a good king. They were married on her eighteenth birthday—it helped to cover up what had happened just a year ago—and he had just turned thirty.

She did pick up a bit after she was married. She never became exactly lively again, but then she was also getting older. Her smiles came more easily, and to her own surprise, she fell in love with her earnest young husband. He had known full well when his marriage proposal had been officially offered and officially accepted that Alora thought of him vaguely as a nice man and she did have to marry someone suitable. He also realized without false modesty that as available royalty went, he was a bargain. Not only did he not wear a corset nor have a red nose, he did have a sense of humor.

So, after he married her, he set out not really to woo her, which he thought would be cheating when affairs of state had almost forced them to get married in the first place, but to be as unflaggingly nice to her as he thought

he could get away with. Their delight in each other after
they became the sort of lovers that minstrels make ballads
about (although it was certainly unpoetic of them to be
married to each other) was so apparent that it spilled
over into their dealings with their people; and the court
became a more joyful place than it had been for many a
long royal generation. And minstrels did make ballads
about them, even though they were married to each other.

It was the tradition in this country that when the King
and Queen reached a certain age—nobody knew precisely
when that age was, but the country was lucky in its monarchs as it was lucky in so much else, and somehow they
always had enough sense to know when they had reached
it—they retired, and the next King and Queen took over.
The older ones always went off to live somewhere as far
away and as obscure as possible so they would not be
tempted to meddle; and the new pair could settle in and
start off without the grief of their parents' death hanging
over them—or the feeling, on the other hand, that the parents were just in the next room, grumbling about the
muddle those youngsters were making.

But usually the old King and Queen did not step down
until the young ones had a child or two, and it half-raised
and at least potentially capable of looking after itself to
some extent. But Alora bore no children. And at last her
parents shrugged and said that they had waited long
enough. The Queen dreamed every night about that little
cottage in the woods, with the brook beside it, and a flower
garden that she could keep with her own hands—sometimes she dreamed of it two or three times in a night. Children weren't strictly necessary, even for monarchs; there

was always somebody available to pass a crown to. And so at last came a day full of boxes and wagons and shouts, and last-minute directions on ruling ("Don't forget that the Duke of Murn expects to be served fresh aradel at every dinner he's invited to: I don't care what season it is, he will make your life miserable with hunting stories if you don't"). It all ended eventually with "Well, don't worry, you won't make too big a mess of it; we have faith in you; and come and visit us sometimes when the garden is blooming—and, well, goodbye."

While the people lined the roads and cheered, the new Queen Alora and King Gilvan stood silently on their balcony, the Royal Balcony of Public Appearances and Addresses, and watched the wagons roll away.

When the wagons were quite out of sight, and only a dusty blur on the horizon remained, hanging over the road they took and greying the trees that lined it, the pair on their balcony turned and went down into the palace, into their private rooms.

Gilvan was the first to break the silence; he sighed and said: "I wish my parents would take it upon themselves to retire. There're more than enough rising generations to take over for them—in fact you'd think the pressure from below would rise up and sweep them away . . . but dukes and duchesses never seem to feel the compulsion to be reasonable that kings and queens do." Gilvan had felt rather than seen the unhappy look Alora had given him when he spoke of rising generations, and he knew what she was thinking before she opened her mouth. "Don't worry about it," he said simply. "You needn't."

"But—"

"I alone have half a dozen brothers and sisters, and they're all married and all have half a dozen children apiece. As your father said—"

"He didn't exactly say it," said Alora hastily.

"No; his range of *hems* is wide and most expressive. But the crown won't go begging; that's all." Gilvan paused and looked thoughtful. "There's rather a glut on the market in royal offspring in our day, really. We don't have to add to it. In fact, it may be wiser that we don't. There isn't all that much for all of us to do. There are too many local festivals and celebrations of this and that already, and even more dukes and earls to do the presiding."

Alora almost laughed. "Yes, but as King and Queen we really ought to have an heir. Of our own."

Gilvan shrugged. "Noisy little beasts, children—or at any rate our family's are all tiresomely loud—we can do without them. There are too many that have to visit us already. And if you mean that direct-line stuff, well, the crown has done more dancing around over the last several hundred years than a cat on a hot stove. A small leap to a nephew —is it Antin that's the oldest? We aren't due for Queen What's-her-name, are we?"

"No, Antin, fortunately. Lirrah is the next oldest."

"And hasn't a brain in her pretty head." Gilvan looked relieved. "I thought it was Antin—as long as he doesn't break his neck out hunting someday. Anyway, a small leap to a nephew won't discomfit it any. And you know I don't mind."

Alora looked at him and nodded: he was only speaking the truth. He didn't mind; but she did not know how much that decision had cost him, and she couldn't help wonder-

ıg. And she did mind, somehow; and she rather thought
hat their people, even if only wistfully, did too. Antin was
nice boy (and let nothing happen to him! One could only
ope Lirrah's parents could find someone with sense
nough for two to marry her), but . . . she didn't mean
ɔ think of Ellian, but still she often did; and she knew
he rumor that was whispered about her, Queen Alora:
hat she bore her husband and her kingdom no children
ɛecause she had never quite recovered from the loss of
ɛer sister years ago. She wasn't sure that this wasn't
orrect.

But then, shortly after she became Queen, and after a
lozen quiet years of marriage, Alora began to have dizzy
pells in the mornings when she first stepped out of bed.
he didn't like being sick, so she ignored them, assuming
hat if they didn't get any attention they would go away;
ɪnd every day they did, but most mornings they came
ɛack. Then other things happened, and she knew for
ure: but she was afraid to tell anyone, because perhaps
t still wasn't true, maybe she read the signs wrong be-
ause she wanted so much that it be true. And then one
lay Gilvan went looking for his wife and couldn't find her
ɪnywhere that he thought she should be; and at last when
ɪe was beginning to feel a little worried, he ran her to
ɛarth in their big bedroom. The bed itself was a monster,
ɪp three velvet-carpeted steps to a dais almost as large as
he dais that held the royal table in the banqueting hall.
The four carved bedposts stood eight feet above the mat-
ress, broad as masts, and were almost black in color,
ɾielding only a very little brown warmth if the sun shone
ull upon them; the bed-curtains were as elaborate as a

hundred of the finest needlewomen could make them
working all day for six months before the royal wedding
a dozen years ago.

Alora looked very small, sitting at the great bed's foot
her arms around one of the posts, her face pressed agains
the curtains. She sat very still, as if she were afraid sh
might overflow if she moved; but with joy or sorrow h
could not tell.

"What is it?" he said, and realized his heart was thump
ing much louder than it ought to be.

She opened her eyes and saw him, and a smile over
flowed her quietness. She let go the bedpost and held ou
her arms to him. "Our heir," she said. "Six months more
I think, if I have been keeping proper count. I've been
afraid to tell you before, but it's true, after all these
years. . . ."

Gilvan, who had never cared before, discovered sud
denly and shatteringly that he was about to care ver
much indeed.

Alora had been keeping proper count; five months and
twenty-seven days later she gave birth to a daughter
while Gilvan paced up and down a long stone corrido
somewhere in the palace—later, he was never quite sur
where it was—and thought about all sorts of things, not a
one of which he could remember afterward. They named
her Linadel, and her christening party was the most mag
nificent occasion anyone could remember. The young
sprigs and dandies of the court—even the best-regulated
court has a few of them who are above having a good time
—had a good time; the great-grandmothers who spent al
their time complaining how much handsomer and finer

and generally superior things had been when they were young unbent enough to smile and admit that this was really a rather nice party, now they came to think of it. And the old King and Queen dusted themselves off, and left their precious flower garden long enough to return to the capital, and meet their new granddaughter, and borrow some fancy dress, and go to the party; and they even thought their granddaughter was worth it.

Linadel herself was rosy and smiling throughout, and didn't seem to mind being kept awake so long and passed from one set of strange arms to another, and breathed on by all sorts (all the better sorts, at least) of strange people. She continued to smile and to make small gurgles and squeaks, and to look fresh and contented. It was her parents who wore out first and called an end to the festivities.

Linadel grew up, as princesses are expected to do, more beautiful every day; and with charms of mind and manner that kept pace. She didn't speak at all till she was three years old, and then on her third birthday she astonished everyone by saying, quite distinctly, as she sat surrounded by gifts and fancy sweets, and godmothers and godfathers (she had almost two dozen of them), and specially favored subjects and servants, "This is a very nice party. Thank you very much." Everyone thought this was a very auspicious beginning; and they were right. Linadel never lisped her r's or took refuge in smiling and looking as pretty as a picture (which she could have done easily) when she tackled a comment too large for her. On her fourth birthday she presented everyone with what

amounted to a small speech. "And a better one than some
I've heard her granddaddy give," said a godfather out of
the corner of his mouth to a godmother, who giggled.

She never looked back, whatever she did. In any other
kingdom her parents and friends—and everyone was her
friend—would have said that the faeries had blessed her.
Here, they said only, "Isn't she wonderful, isn't she beautiful, isn't it splendid that she's ours?"

She *was* beautiful. Her hair was dark, velvet brown by
candlelight and almost chestnut in the sun; and it fell
in long slow curls past her shoulders. When she was
thoughtful, she would wind a loose curl—her thick hair
invariably escaped from its ribbons—around one hand and
pull gently till it slid through her fingers and sprang back
to its place. This habit, as she grew older, made young
men breathe hard.

Her eyes were grey. Or at least mostly grey. They had
lights and glimmers in them that some people thought
were blue, or green, or perhaps gold; but for everyday
purposes (and even a princess has need for a few everyday facts) they were grey. Her skin was pale and pure,
with three or four coppery freckles across her small nose
to keep her from being perfect. Her hands were long
and slim and quiet, and a touch from them would still a
barking dog or soothe a fever.

But the strongest thing about her, and perhaps the
finest too, was her will. It was her will that prevented her
from being hopelessly spoiled, when without it—in spite
of the intelligence and cheerfulness that were as much a
part of her as her dark hair and pale eyes—it would have
been inevitable. Her will told her that she was a princess

and would someday become a queen, and had responsibilities (many of them tiresome) therefore; but beyond that she was an ordinary human being like any other. It was her position as a princess which explained the extravagant respect and praise she received from everyone (except her parents, whom she could talk to as two other ordinary human beings caught in the same trap); and it was this belief in her essential ordinariness that prevented her head from being turned by the other. She did very well this way; and the strength of this willful innocence meant that she did not realize that the respect and admiration was by it that much increased.

It is all very well to say that all princesses are good and beautiful and charming; but this is usually a determined optimism on everybody's part rather than the truth. After all, if a girl is a princess, she is undeniably a princess, and the best must be made of it; and how much pleasanter it would be if she were good and beautiful. There's always the hope that if enough people behave as though she is, a little of it will rub off.

But Linadel really was good and beautiful and charming, and kind and thoughtful and wise, and while at the very end you must add "and wonderfully obstinate," well, for a girl in her position to support all her other virtues, she had to be.

But how to find such a paragon a suitable husband? When she was fifteen her parents began reluctantly to discuss the necessity of finding her a husband. They should have done this long ago, but had put it off again and again. The obvious choice was Antin, who was a nice boy, and who, if Linadel had not been born, would have worn the crown anyway; and the thought that he would not disgrace it had comforted Gilvan and Alora through their childless years. But that comfort was fifteen years old now, and Antin was a man grown—and still, really, a rather nice boy. It was not that he was lazy, for as a duke, and one still in line for the throne although now once removed, he had duties to perform and dignity to maintain, and he performed and maintained suitably. He was also a splendid horseman (a king needs to look good on horseback for the morale of his people) and no physical coward. It wasn't even that he was stupid—although he did have a slight tendency toward royal corpulence. But—somehow—there was something a little bit missing. This was perhaps most visible in the fact that he, while very polite about the honor of it, et cetera, wasn't the least enthusiastic himself about marrying his young and beautiful cousin. Both Alora and Gilvan, trying to see behind his eyes, felt that his attitude toward kingship was one of well-suppressed dislike.

The rumor was that he was in love with a mere viscount's daughter, who was pretty enough and nice enough, but not anything in particular herself, and that the only enthusiasm Antin did feel on the subject of Linadel's marriage was that it should happen soon and to someone else; so that he would be free to marry his little Colly. Gilvan and Alora became aware of the rumor, and by that time they were inclined to hope it was true, as the best for everybody concerned.

But it was delicate ground nonetheless, and if Antin were to be discarded as an eligible king, a better reason than his indifference to the post must be found. This proved more difficult than it looked. It was managed finally, after a lot of hemming and hawing on all sides, with an agreement that since everybody in Gilvan's and Alora's families was already related to everybody else, usually in several different degrees, to add further to the confusion by marrying Linadel to Antin was beyond the point of sense.

Everyone involved breathed a sigh of relief. It can be assumed that this included Colly, although no one asked her.

It was true that the royal family of this kingdom, like those of many other kingdoms, had mostly the same blood running through all of its veins; but if Antin himself had not been a specific problem, the subject probably would not have come up. As it was, it meant that Linadel's husband could not be any other member of the family either. It was a relief to have found a way to reject Antin without losing too much face (and the people talked about it anyway: the true purpose of a royal family, as Gilvan rather often observed, is to be a topic of gossip common to all, and thus engender in its subjects a feeling of unity and shared interests); but one still was left to play by the rules one had made, however inconvenient those rules were.

And, as Gilvan and Alora understood in advance and soon proved in fact, the last mortal kingdom before Faerieland had some difficulty in luring an outsider of suitable rank, parts, and heritage to be its king; even with Linadel as bait—or perhaps partly because of it. The ones who were willing were willing because they were fascinated by the thought of all that stealthy and inscrutable magic, sending out who knew what impalpable influences across its borders which lay so near although no one could say precisely where—an attitude which Alora and Gilvan and their people didn't like at all. Such candidates as there were were almost automatically poets or prophets or madmen, or all three combined; and the first were foolish, the second strident, and the third disconcerting; and none of them would have made a good king.

The rest were afraid, afraid to come any nearer than they already were—which, if they were near enough to receive state visits from that last kingdom, was probably too near.

"I'll marry her to a commoner first!" said Gilvan violently after a particularly unfortunate interview with the fifth son of a petty kingdom who fancied his artistic temperament.

"I've only just noticed something," Alora said wearily; "the only immigrants we ever get—the ones that stay, and seem to love it here as we do—they're never aristocrats. We haven't had any new blue blood in generations. I'd never thought of it before. I wonder if it means anything."

"That aristocratic blood runs thinner than the usual sort," said Gilvan shortly. He drummed his fingers on his purple velvet knee. "Besides, there's no room for them. Why should they come? We have more earls per square foot than any other country I've ever heard of. . . ."

"And we're related to every last one of them," said Alora, and sighed.

It was a problem, and it remained a problem, and two

years passed without any promise of solution. Linadel didn't mind because she had never been in love; the idea of a husband was a rational curiosity only, like how to get through state occasions without treading on one's great heavy robes—and how, in those same robes, heavy and cumbersome as full armor, one could hold one's arms out straight and steady for the Royal Blessing of the People, which took forever, because there were always lots of special mentions by personal request of a subject to his sovereign. She had asked Alora, whose arms never trembled, and Alora had smiled grimly and said, "Practice."

So Linadel practiced being a princess—it wouldn't occur to her that it came to her naturally—and became wiser and more beautiful, and even more loving and lovable; and she wasn't perfect, but she wasn't ordinary either.

There was a hidden advantage to this preoccupation with finding Linadel a suitable husband; it took her parents' minds off the ever present fear all parents of beautiful daughters in that last kingdom felt. Gilvan doted on his daughter and realized furthermore that she really was almost as wonderful as he thought she was; and with a similar sort of double-think he put out of his mind any thought of losing her to Faerieland. He had occasionally to deal with other parents' losses—even a king is occasionally touched by the thing his people keep the most forcefully to themselves—but he refused to apply the same standard to himself. Once he wandered so far as to think, "Besides, an only child is never taken" and recoiled, ap-

palled that he should come to reassuring himself on a
subject by definition unthinkable. And that had been when
Linadel was a child of only a few years.

In the same summer that Gilvan avoided reassuring
himself, Alora and Linadel, wandering far from the royal
gardens, discovered a little meadow whose bright grass
was thick with the mysterious blue flowers that the
people of that country would never gather, that they
called faeries'-eyes. The stems were long and graceful,
each bearing several long slender leaves and a single small
flower at its tip, nodding in breezes that human beings
did not feel, and glowing in the sunlight with a color that
could not quite be believed. It was undeniably blue, that
color, but a blue that no one had ever seen elsewhere.

Linadel ran forward with a cry of pleasure and plucked
one of the flowers before her stunned mother could stop
her: and she ran back at once when Alora failed to follow
her and held the flower up and said, "Isn't it lovely,
Mother? May we take some home?"

Alora, looking down, saw with a terrible pang that
deep ethereal blue reflected in her own daughter's eyes.
But she said only, very quietly, "No, my dear, these are
wildflowers, and they do not like to sit in houses; we will
leave them here." She took the small blue thing Linadel
held and laid it in the grass near its fellows, and they
turned away from that meadow and walked elsewhere.

Alora dreamed of that meadow, and the blue in Linadel's wide grey eyes, for years after that; but she never
remembered the dream when she awoke—only a vague
feeling of fear, and of things forbidden; and she did not
recall the incident that had begun the dreams.

What she did still recall was her sister's face; and some-times the young Linadel reminded her of what Ellian had been at the same age. Linadel's coloring was similar to her aunt's, but there the resemblance ended, beyond a chance fleeting expression such as young princesses every-where may occasionally be caught at. The thing that Alora noticed more and more as the years passed was how much more solemn Linadel was than she and Ellian had been; but Linadel had no sister to help bear the oppressive weight of royalty.

By the time Linadel's seventeenth birthday was the next occasion on the state calendar, she had practiced princessing so successfully that her royal robes never got under her feet any more, nor did her arms tremble; and her mother suddenly realized: "She is preparing to be a queen alone." She thought of Gilvan and how little her life would have been without him, and her heart failed her. And then a new juggler's trick would make the Princess laugh, or a new ballad make her look as young and lovely as she really was—if less like a queen-to-be —and Alora would think, "She's only a girl. It's not fair that she should have to understand so much so soon." And Linadel's smile, and sidelong look to her parents to join the fun, would remind Alora of Ellian again.

The poor Queen's thoughts went round and round, and Linadel's birthday came nearer and nearer; and the pos-sible husbands had petered out to what looked to be the final end. Then one night Alora dreamed of Linadel and the blue flower, and she remembered her dream when she woke up: and she also remembered what she had dreamed after: Linadel had grown up in a few graceful moments as her mother watched, still holding a fresh blue flower, till she was almost seventeen; but then she laughed and opened her arms to embrace Alora, and the Queen realized that it was not Linadel standing before her, but Ellian. She woke sobbing, to find herself in Gilvan's arms, and he smoothed her hair and said, "It's only a dream" till she fell asleep again; but she would not tell him what her dream had shown her. When he asked her, the next morning, she did not meet his eyes as she answered that she could not remember.

Alora was correct in thinking that her daughter was anticipating being a queen without a king to argue official questions and complain of the humorlessness of ministers with. The Princess found being a princess a heavy task, since—as her parents had long recognized—she couldn't help taking her royal responsibilities seriously. She was the only one there was. She had often thought, wistfully, that it would be a very nice thing to have brothers and sisters—as all her cousins did—since being eldest, and heir apparent, couldn't be nearly as bad as being the only one at all. Two years before, when the question of Antin was being discussed, she had also had her first real glimpse of how it was to be where she was as seen from another point of view. This glimpse had left a lasting impression. She had known at once that he wanted no part of her— and known too that his feeling had nothing personal to her in it: it was focused on the position she occupied. And it had come as something of a shock.

She still knew, as she had always known, that she was an ordinary girl; after Antin she also knew that it didn't matter. The princess mattered. And the queen who would eventually reign mattered. And so she took more walks alone, and spent more afternoons—when her political lessons allowed it—in dusty disused towers and forgotten wings of the castle, where she could play hopscotch if she felt like it, and sing silly songs that had hundreds of verses to the resident barn swallows, who didn't mind her in the least. Even this amusement her conscience frequently denied her, or at any rate it took its revenge later by keeping her up late at night studying her country's history, and geography, and biographies of its great men and women; which she found very interesting, but not very relaxing.

In the meanwhile Lirrah married a nice young earl who had earnestness enough for two, at least, if not necessarily brains; and a year later they produced a daughter. Linadel thought to herself: "I'll have to bring her to court when she gets a little older; she may be Queen after me." The royal family attended the christening, of course; and little Silera became Linadel's first godchild. Shortly after that, Antin declared his engagement with the Viscount of Leed's daughter, Colly.

Linadel's seventeenth birthday was going to be a holiday the like of which none had ever seen before—not even the day of her christening would be able to compare with it, and those fortunate enough to remember that occasion were still talking about it. Royal birthdays were always splendid fun anyway; and since the royal family only celebrated two a year, no one ever got bored with them. Gilvan's and Alora's birthdays were only ten days apart, and the celebration was held on the Queen's birthday. "I can wait," Gilvan always said during the annual token argument about it. "I'm twelve years older than you are, what do I care about ten days?"

Linadel's birthday came in early autumn, in that breath of time between harvest and the break in the weather that means winter is only weeks away. The King and Queen began planning for it as soon as their own birthday—which came about the time of the first real thaw in the spring, so that the celebrations were occasionally enlivened by the Nerel River, which ran near the palace and through the town, choosing to overflow its banks, usually over the parade route—was safely past. But the plans for the year that Linadel would be seventeen had a certain desperation to them that no one admitted but everyone felt. Everyone knew—Linadel herself included, though she could not remember having been told, and her mother certainly had never mentioned it to her—that the Queen's only sister had disappeared the morning of their seventeenth birthday; and no one thought it surprising that Alora looked paler than she otherwise ought, that summer before her daughter turned seventeen. She, poor lady, assumed that she hid her fears well enough that none noticed, since none spoke to her of being a little off her looks, and was anything troubling her? And for this kindly conspiracy she was so grateful that she wasn't quite as pale as she might have been.

But far from the palace, far enough away that even a wind-borne whisper could not make the journey, people spoke to each other more openly than they had ever dared when it was merely their own or their neighbors'

children that were threatened. "She is our princess—they
—they could not."

"They will not care for that: she is too beautiful."

"But she is the only one."

"They will not care."

And the plans for the birthday grew more and more
elaborate under the pressure of too much wild energy,
from the love her people had for their only princess.

It was no secret among the royal three that a royal
birthday party was for the pleasure of the people, and a
nuisance to its subject. Alora and Gilvan had always arranged Linadel's for her, even after she was old enough
to take some reluctant interest in it, so that she need be
harassed by no more than the day itself, and not by thinking about it for six months previous. But this year she
took an active part in the plotting and planning, and took
fewer long solitary walks than had been her habit for the
last several years. Alora thought, rather sadly, with the
front of her mind what she had often thought before:
that Linadel was growing up too quickly, whether her
parents would or nay; and was not aware that in the back
of her mind she was relieved to have her only daughter
readily under her eye so much of the time. But Gilvan
understood, and thanked his daughter silently for it; and
Linadel acknowledged his understanding by not meeting
her father's eyes.

The summer months passed, and the preoccupation
with the coming birthday bode fair to turn it into a day
the like of which nobody who had ever lived in any
country could have recalled. There were almost no ju-

dicial cases to be considered, because everyone was too preoccupied either to get into mischief or to complain about their neighbors. Even the court counselors, ministers, and sundry assistants stumbled over their florid phrases and seemed to be thinking about something else; normally endless discussions of precedence and rule between those of opposite persuasions trailed off into vague nods and indefinite adjournments. The scrutiny that Princess Linadel was under spread to include her parents.

King Gilvan, who should have been well into middle age, was still tall and straight and handsome (as befitted Linadel's father); and his devotion to his people was strong enough to force him into a vast and apparently stolid patience, which had not been in his nature at all to begin with; and yet in spite of this he was never bitter, and had retained the tendency of his young manhood to be humorous whenever he thought he could get away with it. Queen Alora was quick and kind, as she had been since she was a child, and grew only a little more fine-drawn and fragile with age, and no less beautiful (as befitted Linadel's mother), but much harder to read; because as she understood more and more about her people, she did not wish to distress them by allowing them to see how much she understood.

And Linadel was hourly more beautiful till even those who had seen her daily since she was a baby were struck by it as if they had never seen her before; although it seemed in latter days that only her father could make her laugh.

The week before the birthday was stretched, minute by minute, as tight as a girth on a straining horse. Even the marketplace was subdued, though usually the echoes of argument and abuse, conversation, flattery, and general cheerfulness flew over the entire town like a flock of birds. Usually it was noisier before a holiday, as everyone made last-minute adjustments in their fancy dress. The Queen had no sleep at all, for whenever she closed her eyes she saw nothing but blue flowers; saw them growing in across the palace windowsills, out of jars on her dressing table, in urns at the high table where they ate their formal meals; and once she saw the scarlet carpet that lay before the thrones in the audience room turn into a field of little blue flowers on stems so tall that they reached the knees of the King and Queen and Princess who sat high above the floor on a carnelian dais.

Gilvan wasn't sleeping too well either, although dreams of blue flowers were not a part of his portion; but when he woke up and looked around, in starlight or moonlight, he could see the glint of the Queen's open eyes as she lay motionless on the bed beside him. Sometimes if he spoke to her she would close her eyes to please him, and try to think of yellow chrysanthemums and white horses and crimson maple leaves until his breathing told her he was asleep again and she could open her eyes.

Linadel, who had originally thought that she was comforting everybody else and especially her mother, found that tension was contagious, and began spending many night hours kneeling on the windowseat and peering out over the broad sill of her bedroom window. It looked out over the vast palace gardens, and the river beyond, and the town beyond that, and behind it the forested hills; and there was a great deal of uninterrupted sky over them all. She looked up, mostly, because she did not want to be reminded of the life she led in those gardens, along that river, and with the people of the town—her people; so she picked out the constellations she had learned when she was a small child, and thought of the stories that went with them. But she was careful to be in bed, and at least apparently asleep, when a lady-in-waiting—whoever was due for the privilege this fortnight—came to wake her in the morning.

The day before the Princess's Day was clear and fine, with a sky of that hard and infinite blue that guarantees good weather for a week following. The town houses were already draped in bouquets of flowers and bright-colored ribbons, and the parade route marked with banners worked with the royal crest, and with great baskets of flower petals—presently covered with tight-fitting lids— that the people who tomorrow would line the way could scatter in their Princess's path. The last sign of preparation would be the royal bodyguards, already dressed in their finest uniforms and glittering with gold braid and the topazes of their office, coming round in pairs to unstrap the baskets.

Alora often went to her daughter's room just before bedtime, and stayed to talk for a few minutes after the current lady-in-waiting in charge of evening preparations had been dismissed and Linadel was brushing and braiding her long smoky hair herself; but this night her mother lingered to tuck her in—which she hadn't done since the eight-year-old Linadel had become sensitive about her dignity—and to sit on the foot of the bed. Neither of them said anything. The sky was blocked from Linadel's sight as she lay back on her pillows, but she watched her mother looking out the window and wondered which Alora's favorite stars were, and if they were the same as her own.

The Queen sighed and stirred, and bent over Linadel to kiss her good night once more. "Sleep well, dear heart. It will be a long day tomorrow, and longest for you." She turned away and left her daughter's room at just the proper pace, and without looking back; as she passed the threshold she cocked her head just a little to one side to suggest casualness, and Linadel's heart went out to her.

Dawn was hardly grey in the sky when Linadel's favorite lady-in-waiting hurried into the Princess's grand bedroom to awaken her young mistress. The parade would begin shortly after the sun was well up, and there was breakfast to be coaxed into her—she didn't like to eat much on these very early mornings, but had learned the hard way that she'd be exhausted by noontime if she did not—and a great deal of dressing and over-dressing and pinning, draping, combing, and last-minute rearranging to be done. The lady was almost as young as her mistress, and hadn't paid too much attention to the fears of her elders about princesses and seventeenth birthdays —which was one reason why Linadel had found her so restful to have around recently. But she was hardly across the threshold when she noticed that Linadel's bed was empty.

She looked around, trying to feel only surprised, trying to think that the Princess had merely awakened already and was waiting for her; but she saw no one. She took the few dreadful steps between her and the bed and stared down at the small blue flowers scattered across the pillow: and then she screamed, screamed again, and wrapped her arms around her body, for it felt as though her heart would burst out; and she turned and hurled herself out of that haunted room.

The Queen could not have heard the waiting-woman's scream, for their room was several corridors away. But a shiver ran through her at that moment nonetheless, and she stood up blindly from where she had been sitting near the window, and went to the Princess's room. Gilvan, who had been awake nearly as long as she, and staring moodily with her at the perfect sky, and the soft sunrise coloring it, with no word exchanged between them, rose up and followed her.

Alora crossed the threshold to her daughter's room first. After the lady-in-waiting had fled, a strange implacable silence, thick as water, had flowed into that room and spread out into the corridor beyond. Alora stood like a statue with her face turned to the Princess's empty bed for just a few moments, long enough for Gilvan to reach her when she put her hands over her face and fainted.

PART TWO

LINADEL HAD NO idea where she was when she woke up; but when she opened her eyes and turned her head, expecting to shrug off the dream that held her, the dream continued. She had thought that it should be the morning of her seventeenth birthday, but . . . even as she thought this the truth of it eluded her. Her mother had sat on the foot of her bed last night . . . hadn't she? She *must* remember her mother.

The pillowslip under her cheek was silk—if it were cloth at all—so soft that it was unimaginable that it had ever been woven: it must have just grown, like a flower. The lace that edged it was a fragile beautiful pattern totally unfamiliar to her: she was sure her fingers had never worked it, nor her mother's nor any of the court ladies'. She did remember with utter certainty that she was a princess: and no royal cheek ever touched a pillowslip of less than aristocratic origins. Her thoughts wavered again. She wished terribly that she could remember her mother's face: not remembering made her feel far more forlorn than any strangeness of her surroundings could do.

She was covered by a long soft fur which was the elusive blue-grey of a storm cloud; and it belonged to no animal she knew. Stroking aside the long fine hairs, she touched the downy fur underneath and knew also that no dyer ever born could mix such a tint.

She looked up. There were trees overhead—or at least she thought they were real trees; their branches met and intertwined so gracefully as to look deliberate, the bright bits of sky scattered more credibly by a painter's inspired brush than by the cheerful haphazard hand of Nature.

It seemed she was in a small meadow, and she lay on the ground on a white sheet spread over an improbably smooth and comfortable piece of greensward; but when she put her hand out and hesitantly touched the blades that sprang out from under the edge of the white cloth upon which she lay, they felt like real grass; and she snapped one off, and rubbed it between her fingers, and the smell was the good green smell she had always known. She closed her eyes and for a moment she almost remembered what her past life had been. She frowned, and her fingers closed down on the grass blades till their sap ran onto her hand; but the memory was gone before she found it. She opened her eyes, and her hand. At least the grass was the same here and wherever she had come from. She was obscurely comforted and looked around her with better heart. She did not realize that with any lifting of spirits in this land her hold on her previous life diminished; already there was only a thread left. That thread was her royalty, for nothing but death could make her forget that. But she did not know, and there was much here to catch her attention.

The trees that surrounded her meadow and met over her head grew to a great height, with the proud arch of branches that reminded her of elms; but the luminous quality of the bark was like no elm she had seen. They stood in a ring around her, although she lay near one edge, the nearest tree being only a child's somersault away, while the one opposite was several bounds distant for the fleetest deer; and she wondered if deer ever came to this graceful tended meadow. Beyond the ring of trees was a hedge: perhaps she was in a kind of ornamental garden; a very grand and ancient garden indeed, that had trees laid out as lesser gardens had flowerbeds, and had been watched over and cared for during so many years that the trees had grown to such a size and breadth. The hedge grew higher than her head, although no more than half the height of the trees; and it was starred with flowers, yellow, ivory, and white; and she thought perhaps they were responsible for the gentle sweet smell that pervaded the air.

There were arches cut through the hedge, each of them tall enough for the tallest king with the highest crown to pass through without bending his head: four arches, as if indicating the four points of the compass. She looked at each of them slowly, and through them saw more close-trimmed grass, and flowers; through the third a fountain stood in the middle of what looked like a rock garden of subtle greys and chestnuts; and through the fourth she saw—people.

She stood up, and the fur coverlet slipped away from her and fell in a noiseless heap at her feet. She found that her heart had risen in her throat and was beating so

hard that she raised her hands as if to force it back down
into her breast where it belonged. Her hands were shaking, and she dropped them; and her heart eventually
subsided of its own accord. She stood looking at the
people for a moment; their clothing was bright as jewelry
in the green glen, and while they were too far away for
her to distinguish faces, they seemed oblivious to her.
She could not see what they were doing, as they moved
back and forth in front of her open door; but there was
something so lucid and precise about them that she was
caught by the fancy of their being stones in some great
necklace, the fastening of which with her dull eyes she
could not quite make out.

Then she looked calmly around her, wondering that
since she was here in her nightgown, perhaps her robe
and slippers were here too. She did not really relish introducing herself to these people she saw brief glorious
bits of through the leaves of the hedge, with her hair
down her back and her feet bare; but she would if she had
to, for join them she must. How she came to be here,
wherever here was, and why, and what she had been
before—this was a thought that still made her unhappy
when she stumbled over it, though the reasons got vaguer
and vaguer—she would deal with later. At the moment,
such thoughts would only make her heart thunder and her
hands tremble again, which was unprincesslike.

She did not find anything that seemed like the robe
and slippers that had belonged to her—she was pretty
sure they were blue and silver—but near where her feet
had lain was something magnificently red, dark heart's-
blood red, now tangled negligently with the pale fur.

When she picked it up it shook itself out into a long gown with a waterfall of a skirt and narrow sleeves edged with gold; and under it had been hidden small gold shoes with soles as tender as the soft grass. She put the dress on with great care, and laced the golden laces at waist and wrists; and put her feet in the golden shoes. She pulled her hair free of its braid, and shook it out, combing it with her fingers till it fell, she thought, more or less as it usually did; but she had nothing to put it up with. She shrugged, and it rippled down her back and mixed with the folds of her skirt.

Then she walked, slowly, still half in her dream and half somewhere else that she could not remember, toward that arch in the hedge through which she saw the people. Just as she reached it she paused to pluck a flower, a white one, to give herself something to do with her hands besides hiding them in her skirt. She twirled it by the stem and its perfume fanned her face. She took a deep breath and stepped through the door of the hedge.

The people turned their faces toward her at once: and yet there was nothing abrupt about their gesture, nothing of a group startled by a stranger, nothing suspicious or hostile in their wide and serene gaze. Several of the women curtsied; some were standing already, others rose to do so; and some of the men bowed. And again there was so much grace in their movements, and their greeting was so spontaneous, that Linadel no longer felt alone, or even uncertain: she was a member of this kind and courteous group. She did not know these people, and yet there had never been a time when she was not a part of them.

She smiled back to their smiles, and then looked around her, as she was perfectly free to do because she belonged here. She had stepped through the opening in the hedge to find herself in a clearing surrounded by another hedge; and this hedge too was pierced with doorways into more meadows, green with grass and trees and bright with flowers and fountains and warm sleek rocks. In the meadow in which she now stood there was a ring of trees even taller than that which she had just left; and again their branches met and mingled high overhead so she could not see the sky except as scattered bits of blue, irregular as stars in a green heaven.

This meadow was several times larger than the one which she had left; so while there were a number of people in it, and all of them well dressed and proud, and each of them an individual to recognize and respect, the effect was still of peace and quiet and space.

She had walked a few steps forward as she looked, and she realized that more people were entering this ring of trees through the several arches in the hedge; no one was either oppressively still nor visibly restless, but as the minutes passed, Linadel felt that they were waiting for something; and that she was waiting too. Unconsciously she tucked the flower she held into her bodice; and her hands fell peacefully to her sides.

No one had spoken a word, to her or to each other; but the silence was so easy she had thought nothing of its remaining unbroken, despite the slowly increasing numbers of these handsome clear-eyed people. But now a group of musicians had collected at one edge of the clearing and begun to play a high thin tune on flutes and pipes and strings, a tune that seemed somehow woven of the silence that had preceded it. The tune wandered over a wide and many-colored countryside, as the long-eyed bard who must first have played it wandered. Linadel could almost see him—almost—in his grey tunic and high soft leather boots wound round and crossed with long leather laces. Even more clearly she could see the country he traveled: it was a broad, rolling, welcoming country; and every dip of meadow, every small grassy hollow held small blue flowers that nodded and tossed their heads from the tops of their long slender stems.

As she listened, what the music showed her lost her for a moment from the ring of trees and the people she stood among; and so he was only a few steps away from her when she shook herself free of the green-eyed bard and saw him.

"Welcome," he said, and smiled: it was a smile he had never offered to anyone before, a smile he had saved only for her, knowing that someday he would find her; and he held out his hand.

Linadel understood that smile at once, and put her hand in his; and the music changed so that the trees became pillars of sea-colored nephrite, white jade, and cloudy jasper; and the grass and flowers were a shining floor of pale agate and marble and chalcedony; and they were dancing, and all the other people turned each to another, and all were dancing with them.

He was the most beautiful thing she had ever seen; and if her feet had not known what they were doing themselves, she must have tripped and stumbled. He was half a head taller than she, so that she had to tip her head back to look at him; and the strong golden line of his chin almost prevented her from raising her eyes any farther.

His hair was black, so black that any light that fell upon it hid itself at once within the fine heavy waves and was never seen again. It was just long enough to touch the nape of his neck, to tumble over the tops of his ears, to brush his forehead; a tall broad forehead above eyes so blue that nothing else ever again could claim that color's kinship. And those blue eyes were staring down into the upturned face of the most beautiful creature they had ever seen; and their owner was thinking that if his feet were not capable of looking after themselves, surely he would have tripped and stumbled.

Linadel had no idea how long they continued thus, with the glimmering floor beneath them and the glowing pillars around them weaving rainbows in each other's hair. Her ears heard nothing but the elegant warp and tender weft of the music; but still they spoke to each other about everything that mattered. When the music stopped at last, their understanding was complete.

The sudden silence was as gentle and sympathetic as the music had been. Linadel noticed that once again she was standing in a circle of tall trees, and her feet pressed grass and small spangled flowers. It was not like waking from a dream as she stopped and turned and looked around her, but as if she stepped from one dream to the next; and he was still with her, standing beside her, holding her hand.

They faced an arch in the hedge that, now she looked at it, was taller and broader than the others, and outlined in large flowers with long drooping petals of a

subtle violet; their stems were almost turquoise. Linadel
was sure the arches had all been the same size when she
first looked at them, just as she was certain that the sur-
rounding trees had formed a ring, whereas now it was
obviously an oval, with the violet arch at one narrow edge.

Two people stepped through that arch: a man and a
woman. The man looked very much like him Linadel had
just danced with, although his face was graver and the
straightness of his shoulders suggested the strength to
carry burdens rather than the careless strength of youth.
Linadel was also sure that his eyes were less blue than
her partner's; they could not possibly be as blue.

The woman was tall and slender; her face was so
beautiful that it almost hurt to look at her. It was not the
beauty that gave pain, but the serenity that rested within
it, like a raindrop in a flower. Her hair was dark, her
eyes the color of woodsmoke; and Linadel loved her at
once.

A long train of people followed these two, who paused,
it seemed, just inside the threshold of the flowered hedge;
but however many people came in and spilled to each
side in vivid silken and jeweled waves, the grassy clearing was still uncrowded. At last all were inside, and for
a moment all was motionless; and then the beautiful dark
woman swept forward, and the falling shadows of the
brocade she wore were as rich and lovely as any cloth
Linadel had ever seen. She caught Linadel's free hand in
both hers and smiled, and she said: "Welcome. We are
so happy to have you here."

Then the man who stood at Linadel's side and held her
hand raised it and kissed it, and said: "I am named

Donathor; and these are my father and mother, the King of this land, and the Queen."

The King smiled almost as sweetly as his son; and he too kissed her hand and said, "Welcome."

"Donathor is our eldest son," said the dark Queen, "and so he will be King after his father; when we leave you to cross the mountains and grow flowers in a quiet garden. You will be Queen, and we will come back at least once, for the christening of your first child, and bring you armsful of flowers, flowers that only our mountain air and water can produce.

"You will meet Donathor's brothers soon; but we have no daughters, much to our sorrow, and so our welcome to you is even greater than it would be to our eldest son's chosen wife." She caught her breath and opened her big eyes wide and for a moment she looked as young as Linadel; yet this woman's beauty had no age, and it was hard to imagine her being able to count her life in years. But her eyes were as soft as a child's as she said, "I am so pleased to have a girl to talk to again." And her smile was a girl's, and Linadel smiled back, and opened her mouth and heard herself saying something at last; and that something was just, "Thank you. Thank you very much."

But as she spoke she turned back to Donathor, who stood looking down at her as if he had never looked away since he had first taken her hand to dance with her; and perhaps he had not.

Two more people approached: young girls, perhaps Linadel's age. It was hard to assign anybody an age, Linadel thought, looking around her again. The King looked older than Donathor, yes, she could say that, but it seemed more a state of mind than anything she could see. The King's skin was as golden as his son's, and his black hair had no grey in it.

So these young girls, if they were young girls, approached; and they were carrying a golden veil between them, a veil so light that it was hard to see until they were quite near. They threw it over Linadel, and it settled around her like a fine mesh of fire, and as a delicate gold veining on her white skin. When she shook her head to toss her hair back it ran over her shoulders like water, and Donathor had to squeeze his free hand close to his side to keep it from burying itself in those dark gold-flecked waves.

"Hail," said the two girls, their eyes shining like the golden veil. "Hail to Donathor and his bride, the next King and Queen! Hail Donathor and hail Linadel!"

And the rest of the people in that glen took it up, and the shout swung through them like music, and they tossed it over their heads like a ball.

Two more girls appeared, carrying long golden ribbons, and handed the two ends to the girls who had carried the veil, who now stood on either side of the little royal group of four: and then the ribbon was unwound, and the happy crowd stepped forward, and many white hands reached out to hold it; and soon a gold-edged path lay before them, stretching straight through the arch where the King and Queen had entered, and on and on, till Linadel could only see the people as blurs of color with two bits of thin gold unwinding swiftly before them, a strip of green between the gold, and greenness behind them. The ribbon stretched so far that she could no longer recognize it as golden; it was a sparkle of light and a boundary, the end of which she could not see. "Hail!" The cry still went near them, and then it was taken up by more and more people who stepped forward to seize the swift narrow gold. "Hail to the next King and Queen!"

Then a silence swept back to them again, from where the gold ribbons must finally have halted, and it was a silence of waiting. The faces turned back toward the royal four, smiling and joyous faces, waiting for Donathor and Linadel to take the first step, so that the cry could be taken up again and thrown before them to where the end of the golden ribbons awaited them. They waited, smiling and expectant, and the King and Queen turned and bowed to their son and their new daughter, and stepped back for the young pair to precede them.

But Linadel turned a troubled face to her love, and she opened her mouth to speak, but could not think what she must say, and took instead several panting breaths that hurt her. "My parents," she said at last, as if her lips could hardly form the words. "My parents, and my—my people. They are not here." She could not help a rising inflection at the last, and she looked around at the people before her, not sure that they were not after all whom she meant—her people. They *were* her people—she knew it; and yet . . . again she tried to conjure up a picture of her mother's face, and again she could not; and even that, now, told her what she did not want to know. "My parents," she said at last, again, dully. "They must be here, and—I do not see them." In the silence that soft mournful sentence walked as straight down the gold-edged path as any foot might step; and as the people heard it as it passed them their hands dropped, and the golden ribbon drooped. An almost inaudible sigh rose up and pursued the sentence, and caught it, and wrapped it round.

But only silence answered Linadel, and she shook herself free of Donathor's blue eyes and tried to look at him as if his were only a face like other faces and she said: "Where are my parents?" and it was a last appeal. Then suddenly she found herself free of something that had held her till now, although she had not known she was held; and in her new freedom she trembled where she stood. She remembered her mother, and her father, and she remembered herself, and her people, her own people, whom she had known and loved for seventeen years; and she knew they were not the people who held the golden ribbons.

It was the dark Queen who answered her at last: "Child, they are not here."

Linadel stared at that serene and lovely countenance and saw the serenity flicker, like the shadow of a butterfly's wings over a still lake. Then she asked the question to which she now, terribly, knew the answer, and as she spoke she knew she was pronouncing her own doom: "Where am I?" she said.

The King answered her: "You have called it Faerieland. We have no name for it; it is our home."

There was a long, long silence, or perhaps it only seemed so because of the way it sounded in her ears, like the heavy air of a long-closed cavern, that seems to thunder in the skull. At last she said, and her words echoed as though reflected off harsh dark walls of stone, "I must go back. I am the only one there is." And as she said *only one there is*, she felt them all move away from her, as if she were a thief; and another sigh passed over the crowd, but this one was like the rising wind before a storm, moaning and uneasy and warning of things to come.

Perhaps it was only the tears in her eyes that made the golden ribbons heave and tumble and finally fall to the earth, where they lay as still as death, dimming like the scales of a landed fish. She did not know for certain because she turned away as they fell the last way from the hands that had proudly held them high so short a time before; and she put one foot out, and lowered it again till it touched the ground—then the other foot. This land she had determined to leave seemed to fall away from her with even her first unwilling step; it fled so fast it burned her eyes even while she tried not to see. She clasped her empty hands, and heard the last echo of her words flash around her: *the only one there is.*

Two steps gone when she heard his voice, saying, "Wait." She could not help it. Perhaps she meant to, but she could not. She waited.

He took the two steps after her so that he was beside her again, looking down at the bent dark head with its golden tracery, and he said, "I will come with you." He took a piece of the golden net in his fingers and gently stripped it away from his love; and she felt it lift away with surprise, for she had forgotten that she wore it. But when he let go of it, it was too light to fall, and hung like a golden cloud between the two of them and his parents and his people; and so he took his farewell of them with his eyes and their faces glinting with gold; but his mother's tears may have been gold anyway.

"No," said Linadel—"oh no, you cannot." But she could not stop herself from looking at his face one last time, so she looked up as she spoke and what she saw made her silent, for she saw at once that he was changed, changed so that he might go with her, changed so that he must. And she wondered if he too had shed something that had held him as it had held her; or whether he was now caught who had been free before. She shivered as she looked at him, and the golden cloud shivered a little in the air behind them.

The King and Queen held each other's hands as they watched the son they were losing; but they said nothing, and made no move to stop him. Perhaps they understood: perhaps they had seen the change come over him, or known that it must come. They understood at least that there was nothing to say; the King's face had never been so grave. But just before Donathor turned away for the very last time, his father lifted his hand in a sad sketch of the royal blessing; and a little serenity slipped back to his mother's face among the golden tears, and she almost smiled.

Then Donathor turned away and found Linadel's hand once again, and they walked through the opposite arch in the hedge, the one farthest from that through which the golden ribbons had passed. This arch was low and green, and almost shaggy with drooping leaves, and it seemed very far away.

Neither of them had any idea of where they were going; they each knew that their direction was *away*, and that they were together, and for the moment that was enough. They had won through much to be together, and they had earned the right to rest in that knowledge for a little while. Each recalled that last look on the other's face before they had turned toward the arch in the hedge; and while their eyes remained on the path before them and their feet carried them away, one unconsidered step after another, they saw and thought only of each other.

It was Linadel who had the first separate thought, and that thought was: "I wonder if *away* is enough? I've never heard that Faerieland begins anywhere. Or ends," the thought went on, "or that anyone from . . . my side ever crosses that border more than once." She could not feel lost with Donathor beside her, but her thoughts carried her forward like her feet until she met the worst one of all: "I have forced my choice on him." This thought grew and towered over all the rest until it almost blotted out that last look on his face; and then a new little one slipped out from the shadows and confronted her: "Could I have left him? At last . . . would I have gone?"

She stopped with the whispers of this last thought in her ears, and he stopped too, and looked down at her, and read in her eyes what she was thinking. He smiled a little sadly, and after a moment he said: "We have my parents' blessing. We mustn't linger now; we seek yours."

Then Linadel realized what he had known since the first shadow fell upon her and she turned away from the golden ribbons: they were going into exile. Her parents would have to give them up as his had; it was too late for any other choice to be made. For the reasons that the Crown Prince of the immortals loved the Crown Princess of the last mortal land, and she him, the shining things they had seen in each other's faces and read in each other's hearts as they danced together; even for the reasons that neither of them had found someone to marry before, they were bound to each other forever. That was done, past; and thus when she remembered that she belonged to a world other than his, he could no longer belong fully to his own. And no one can belong to two worlds.

No one, mortal, immortal, or creatures beyond the knowledge of either, can belong to two worlds. This was the change she had seen in him when he came after her.

And so, when they had her parents' blessing—and she knew now that they would receive it, for it would be the last thing her dear parents would be able to do for their daughter—they would look for a new world. Perhaps it would be a world like the minstrel's she had seen, striding over green hills that were always the same and always different. "How did you find me?" she thought, and he answered: "I saw you in the water of the rivers that flow from your lands to ours; I heard you in the wind that blew in your window before it blew in mine." "But you did not know my world," she thought. "No," his reply came; "I knew nothing of your world."

They walked on until it grew dark; and Linadel, at last, realized she was tired, and had to stop. By the last rays of the sun they found a tree whose branches hung low under the weight of round yellow fruit; and a stream ran beside the tree. Linadel sat down with a sigh, and they ate the sweet fruit and drank the cold water, and watched the sky over the trees turn rosy, and fade to amber touched with grey; and then black at last, and when Linadel turned her head she could see his profile against the dark trees only because she could remember how it went. She fell asleep sitting up, while he, not accustomed to sleep or the need for it, thought about how he had lived till now, and what would come to him next, and how Linadel had always been a part of everything. Her head nodded forward, and he caught her in his arms as she crumpled to the grass.

When Alora awoke at last, Gilvan saw with a relief that made his knees bend that she was still Alora: her gaze was weak but clear, and she looked around for him at once, knowing that he would be there. He sat down abruptly on the edge of their bed, and when she felt for his hand it was as cold and strengthless as hers. They felt each other's blood begin to flow again in the touching palms; but with the blood came tears: Linadel, their Linadel, was gone.

"We will look for her," Alora said at last. "We must look for her. No one has ever thought to look."

Gilvan thought about this; in the long narrow well of their grief, it seemed perfectly reasonable, and that no one had ever sought a faerie-stolen child before was irrelevant. "Where shall we begin?"

Alora sat up. "I will show you. Where are my clothes?"

Her ladies-in-waiting, then the gentlemen of the King's Inner Chambers, then the courtiers, ministers, special ambassadors, Lords of the King's Outer Chambers, Ladies of the Royal Robes and Seals, visiting noblemen and their families—who were a little slower than the rest to hear about anything that happened since they were unfamiliar with palace routine—and at last even the pageboys, the downstairs servants, and the entire kitchen staff, none of whom had ever thought to question their monarchs in the slightest detail hitherto—all protested vehemently, desperately, when the King and Queen emerged from their private bedroom and, pale but composed, declared that they were going in search of their daughter.

They were dressed as though they might be a wood-cutter and his wife, except that each wore the gold chain of office that a king or queen was expected to wear (except in the bath) until the day each retired. The Keepers of the Wardrobe, even through their sorrow, were startled that the King and Queen could even find such plain clothes to put on.

"No good will come of this," all wailed at them, forgetting in their grief that they were daring to disagree, even hysterically disagree, with their sovereigns. "No good will come of anything that has to do with the faeries," all said, weeping and pulling their hair and patting at the Queen's skirts and the King's knees. "What if we lose you too?" The last was at first a murmur, since these people, like people everywhere, believed that bad luck—which in this land meant faeries—may come to investigate discussions of bad luck; but it took hold, and more and more of the grief-mad palace residents gave up, and spoke it aloud, and it swelled till it might have become a panic.

"There is nothing to suggest that you are going to," said

the King, patiently, or at least nearly so; and the Queen, who perhaps understood despair a little better than her husband, said, "Those who are so upset at the idea that they can't stay home may come with us; but only on the condition that they will be quiet."

Gilvan gave his wife only one brief weary look at this, but he could follow the sense behind it, so he said merely: "You will have a very long walk of it, anyone who does come."

But the King's patience and the Queen's tenderness, which were perhaps a little obviously delivered as to a crowd of foolish children, had their effect. There was a pause as everyone looked at everyone else, and Alora and Gilvan resignedly overlooked them all. "Let me at least make you some sandwiches," said the Chief Cook, at last; and she wiped her eyes on her white apron and disappeared below. Most of her undercooks and assistants slowly detached themselves from the crowd and followed her; and those who remained sat down, and most of them put their heads in their hands. A few spoke to their particular friends in low tones, and several went to the kitchens themselves to ask that they be provided with sandwiches too. A great many of these were made at last, and put in knapsacks with apples and other food that might reasonably survive being banged about in pockets and on shoulders; and some clever person suggested that everybody should bring a blanket—and when the King and Queen finally set out, about twenty of their court, all of whom were excellent walkers, went with them. Alora and Gilvan carried their own bundles, and such was

the morale of the party that no one dared try to seek that
honor for themselves.

Alora led them to the meadow where she and Linadel
had seen the small blue flowers years ago. They startled a
small herd of aradel, which fled silently, eyes wide and
tails high, veering away from the forest directly ahead
of them and entering the trees at the royal party's right
hand. Alora stood at the center of the meadow and turned
her head first one way and then the other as if she were
listening; Gilvan stood near her, hands in pockets, staring
at the sky and squinting, but more, it seemed, at his
thoughts than at the sunlight. "This way," she said at
last, and led the royal herd into the forest also; but not
the way the aradel had gone.

They were deep in the woods when the light began to
fail them, and they made a camp of blankets and addressed themselves to the sandwiches. There was a tiny
stream that twisted through the trees near where they
lay; the water was sweet, and with patience one could
fill a water-bottle. The King himself built a fire and lit it
—and it burnt. Everybody was impressed, which did not
please Gilvan: he knew perfectly well he could build a
proper fire that would burn, and continue to burn, and
not splutter and smoke, even if he was a king. Somebody
produced some packets of tea, and somebody's friend
turned out to be wearing a tin pot, suitable for boiling
water in, under his curiously shaped hat.

The King and Queen retired a little apart, cupping
their hands around the warmth of the tea; the fire was
flickering and subsiding into embers, and everybody was

choosing a tree to lean against, and roots to get comfortable among, if possible, and dropping off to sleep.

"This is the right way," said Alora. "I think."

Gilvan nodded.

"You think so too, then?"

"Not exactly. I feel as though I could tell if it was the wrong one. But I wish I knew where our right way was leading us."

"So do I." Alora sounded so young and woebegone that Gilvan told her almost sharply to finish up her tea and go to sleep. They both lay down and each regulated his or her breathing to make the other one think he or she was asleep; but each lay awake for a long time.

It was Gilvan who woke first, in the first thin and hesitant light of dawn; he started another fire with only a very little mumbling under his breath, by which time a sleepy courtier had stumbled up to fetch the water-boiling pot and gone off to the stream to fill it.

Alora was still asleep. Gilvan looked down at her for a moment, then looked up to watch the only-slightly-more-awake-now courtier set up the pot full of water in a fashion that would give it a fair chance of coming to a boil. He succeeded at last, and sat back on his heels to watch that it didn't change its mind and topple over on him. It would take three potfuls to make tea for everybody; he sighed. He had rubbed his face and eyes with the cold water of the stream, but it only made his skin tingle. His brain was still asleep.

Gilvan turned away and for no particular reason made his way to the little brook and began walking downstream. He thought he might waste a little time till the water would be hot, and it was easier not to think about Linadel if he kept moving. His eyes were on his feet, and his hands in fists, dug into his pockets, and jingling anything he might find there—an absent-minded habit he had had all his life, which ruined the cut of his trousers and reduced the royal tailors to despair. They had finally stopped making pockets for those trousers where the royal dignity could not bear bulges. Gilvan, in his woodcutter's rig, was dimly aware of the luxury of having pockets, but even these thoughts he kept carefully suppressed. The stream widened as he walked. He paused at last, thinking he should turn around and go back; and he looked up.

There was a tiny clearing, no more than the space two or three trees would need, beside the stream just ahead of him; and there he saw his daughter, smiling in her sleep, with her head in the lap of a young man. He was looking down at her when Gilvan first saw them; but something caused him to look up: and their eyes met.

Gilvan knew at once what sort of creature it was whose eyes met his. For a moment he stopped breathing, and he felt that his pulse paused in his veins, his hair stopped growing, and he had no sense of the ground pressing against the bottom of his feet, or the sunlight on his shoulders. This was nothing like the sensation he had had once out hunting, when his horse put its foot in a hole and threw him; and he, dazed and full-length on the ground, found that the boar they were chasing had turned and was grinning at him, the foam dripping from its mouth. It was nothing like the feeling he'd had when Alora smiled at him the first time, either; or when he had been alone with his daughter and seen her take her first

steps without assistance; or when he was sixteen years
old and his favorite godfather died. What he felt now was
nothing like any of these, and yet it was those things that
he remembered.

He came back from wherever he was and looked again
at this young man; only this time he looked beyond the
stillness, the pause of time that Gilvan had felt within
himself, that had told him what he knew: and he saw the
love and tenderness this young man felt for Linadel that
he, Gilvan, had interrupted with his presence. And beyond
that he saw a flicker of something else, something Gilvan
saw was utterly new and strange to this young man: fear.
This fear was the oldest fear of mankind, that the present
does not last; and with that flicker of fear the stillness
wavered too, and a little sense of time, of the passage of
days and years, slipped into the gap, and settled on the
young man's face; and Gilvan found himself thinking,
"This boy is only a few years older than Linadel." Then
Gilvan understood what this meant; and his awful sympathy for someone first learning of time started his breath
again, and his heart, and once again he knew the sunlight
was warm. The young man, still deep in his new knowledge, saw the sympathy, though he did not yet understand it; and he made his beloved's father a shaky smile;
and Gilvan took a step forward.

That step made no sound, yet Linadel was awake at
once and flew to her father, and they hugged each other
till they could hardly breathe. When Gilvan looked up
again, the young man stood a few steps away, hesitating;
and Gilvan gave him a real smile, and letting his daughter
just a little bit loose from the grip in which he still held

her, offered his hand. "This is Donathor," said Linadel to
her father's rough shirt front, and Donathor took the hand;
and Gilvan truly meant the welcome, for Linadel's heart
beat as it always had, and yet a little more warmly; and
her voice was as clear as it had always been, but there was
a new undercurrent of joy in every word. Gilvan her
father relaxed and was happy in this present moment that
had found him his lost daughter; Gilvan the lover remembered Alora's first smile to him, and heard its echo in
Linadel's pronouncing the name *Donathor*, as he had
seen it in the young man's eyes just a little while before;
and for this too he was glad for the present, a trembling,
precarious, yet peaceful bit of time, because it had sad-
dened him no less than Alora that Linadel should face
her life alone, and be resigned to it.

"*Linadel,*" breathed a voice; and she flung herself from
her father's arms only to turn to her mother's. Alora smiled
at Donathor, and there was understanding in her eyes,
but no constraint; and Gilvan thought ruefully that if she
had found them first, she would have felt no difficulty at
all. "How easily we welcome her back," he thought, watching his wife's and daughter's faces and thinking how much
they were alike, and how little; "we hadn't lived with our
grief long enough to believe in it. We were sure we could
find her and bring her back. . . ." He looked again at
Donathor and found him watching Alora with a slightly
puzzled expression on his face, as if he groped for a recol-
lection he could not quite grasp. "Puzzled?" thought Gilvan, puzzled in his turn.

"There will be tea by the time we go back," said Alora,
as if the four of them had been for a quiet walk before

breakfast and were returning to the palace. "And there are plenty of sandwiches left."

Linadel thought of the fruit tree that had provided them their supper the night before, and she looked around for it; but it was not there. The rocks that parted the water of the stream lay in different places than she remembered them from the evening before; and the trees around her . . . were not the same trees. She shivered a little, and knew that she had come home. Then she remembered that it was no longer home, and she hung her head, pretending to gaze at a squirrel that was sitting at the foot of a tree very near them, debating within itself if it dared dash by them. But her parents saw the change of mood in her, and their happiness faltered without their knowing why; and then, before she opened her mouth to begin to explain, they did know why, and their sigh was the sigh of the people who had held the golden ribbons. Donathor stood a little apart from them, the parents and their only child, but she felt his awareness of her, and the strength he tried to offer her through the soft sweet air of that small clearing; and her courage returned, although her sorrow was not lessened by it.

She raised her head and looked at her father and mother in turn, and she knew that they knew already what she was about to say; but that still they waited for her to say it. "I cannot stay here," she said. "Donathor and I are going away—as far away as we can, till we find a country like neither of those we are leaving; and we know we may not find such a land, but we are doomed to the search. We cannot stay here, as we could not stay in his— his parents' land."

As she spoke she looked beyond those she spoke to, at the strange tree that stood where the fruit-laden tree had been; and she wondered again how such things as boundaries were arranged, and she heard her own words: *we cannot stay*, and even as she said them she cringed away from them, although she knew she had no choice but to do as she had said they must. And she saw little glints of sunlight through the green leaves of that tree, and she seemed to see the branches bend a little lower, and phantom yellow globes of fruit hanging from them. The trees murmured together as friends will as they make room for one another, and are joined by those who have been absent; and through this shifting, swaying, half-seen wood she glimpsed something else: a tall hedge pierced with arches, arches so tall that the tallest king in his stateliest crown could pass through any without bending his head; and the arches were outlined with flowers. She was not sure of the hedge because she was not sure of the impossible trees and the transparent fruit; but then she noticed one arch in particular, and was certain that the flowers around it were violet, with stems of lapis lazuli; and she saw people approaching that arch, and passing through it, coming toward herself and Donathor and her parents; and of them she was sure beyond doubt. She and Donathor had left them only yesterday.

Alora and Gilvan saw them too. Gilvan took his hands out of his pockets. The royal tailors needn't really have worried, except for their own pride of craft; Gilvan looked like a king even when he should have looked like a woodcutter with baggy pants, as Alora could only be a queen, even in a partridge-colored dress and heavy boots.

"Wait," said the King who approached them, for he was no less obviously a king than Gilvan. "Wait. We shall not lose our children so—and you will help us." His Queen had suddenly stopped, and stood staring, as humble and innocent as a lost child. Gilvan felt rather than saw Alora take a step forward, and he almost did not recognize her voice as she said:

"Ellian."

And the Faerie Queen burst into tears and ran to put her arms around her long-lost sister.

Those whom Alora and Gilvan had left behind at the palace spent a long, grim day, pecking at their work and at each other, and trying not to think about anything. The royal party had left quietly, winding its way through the palace gardens—which could go on forever if you did not know how to find your way—slipping out at last through a small ivy-rusted side door; and no one was conscious of having mentioned their departure to anyone else. It was as though the ban on speaking of their elusive neighbors had reached out and instantly engulfed those who dared not only to admit their existence openly but to go in search of them, apparently expecting to find them.

But while the countrymen the King and Queen passed on their way to the Queen's remembered meadow asked no question, and while those in the palace sent no messages, somehow by the time the sun set, there were few in that land who did not know that the King and Queen had followed their daughter into the unknown. It was a very quiet evening; no one could think of anything worth discussing, and everyone went to bed early. Even the retired King and Queen felt in their forest that something was not right, although they spoke to no one but each other; and the flowers in their garden drooped, and the shadows that the petals cast were dusty grey instead of black.

The next morning was dull with heavy clouds, and the farmers went grudgingly to tend dull grey fields, and the craftsman unshuttered their dull grey shops; and the wives in their kitchens were cross, because the dough they had set out the night before had failed to rise.

But the sun broke through as the morning lengthened, and the clouds lost their stranglehold on the sky, and even the people's hearts lightened, although they would have been ashamed to admit it; and they watched the clouds break into pieces and drift across the sky till they were mere wisps. People blinked and smiled at one another again, tentatively, because they still preferred not to think about anything too closely.

Then the first and fleetest of the children from the out-lying villages came breathless to the palace, but no one believed them at first; even the brightness of their eyes, the irrepressible joy that stared out from their rumpled hair and the folds of their clothing did not convince the cautious city-dwellers of the truth of the story they told. Not even the crowns and necklaces of blue and yellow and white and lavender flowers they wore were convincing. But their parents came soon behind them, jogging on foot or riding on shaggy plough horses with flowers tangled in their thick manes; and these horses seemed to have forgotten their ploughs, for they lifted their feet like the daintiest of carriage ponies and flicked their tails like foals. The road to the palace was soon crowded with laughing shouting people, and the white dust hung so thick in the air that flower petals tossed overhead hung suspended in it; and it smelled as sweet as the fruit-seller's stall the morning of market day.

The news these flower-mad mortals carried was lost in the tumult; but all those people who had heard nothing the night before, and had gone to bed early and grudged the morning, all of them found themselves washing their hands and changing their shirts, putting on their hats, and making their way to the palace, where something was happening, something splendid; and they went, and they were caught up in the sudden holiday. Not a store could boast its proprietor still within doors; not only the schoolchildren crawled through the windows to join the throng, but their teachers tucked up their skirts and their trouser-cuffs and followed them, not remembering the existence of doors at all.

The old King and Queen found all their flowers nodding firmly in the same direction; and they sighed, but not very much, for something had crept into their hearts too that made them eager to go; and so they began the long walk back to the palace where they had spent so much of their lives, for the second time since their retirement.

And at last into the city came its King and Queen, and its Princess; but the Queen held by the hand another Queen, who smiled a smile brighter than the flowers that hung in the air, and a smile that many found strangely familiar, but they could not pause long enough to wonder at it. Alora held Gilvan's hand on her other side, and the dark Queen held the hand of her King. When the people

waiting for them saw them, a shout went up even louder
than before, and no one felt the least hoarse, although they
had already been shouting most of the morning. How
handsome the four of them looked, walking side by side,
their own beloved King and Queen, and the strange pair
too: you need only look into the eyes of the dark Queen
and know at once that she was to be trusted, as the eyes
and the mouth of the strange King told the same story
of him.

Only Gilvan waved; Alora's hands were full, and the
other King, who also had a hand free, felt that some intro-
duction was necessary before he acknowledged the cheers
of a people who didn't know yet what they were cheering
at. There was no one in that crowd who had the least inclination to find fault with anybody just then, and they
loved him for his smiles, and thought nothing of his not
waving, just as no one thought of Gilvan as dressed like a
woodcutter, with flints and bits of twigs making lumps in
his pockets, or of Alora's scuffed boots.

Behind them came the twenty who had accompanied
Alora and Gilvan on their fools' quest only the day before;
and with them a hundred more, strangers, who carried
flowers, yellow, white, blue, and violet, and wove them in
chains and tossed them to the crowd. They felt no shyness
about their anonymity; they waved and smiled and called
back to the people who called to them, although no one
knew what words were exchanged. The twenty of the
court were the most flower-bedecked of anyone, and they
linked arms and walked four abreast like an honor guard,
except their grins gave them away.

Then at the end of this train was a space that none of

the crowd seemed inclined to fill; and you could see underfoot a carpet of flowers and white dust, and green leaves and sifted pollen. Then, behind this, came Linadel and a strange young man whose beauty and presence were perhaps even equal to that of the Princess; and the crowd gasped and for a moment was silent, and then a new shout went up, but this time, for the first time, there was no question what the people cried:

"Long live the new Queen and her King!"

Even triumphal marches end, and the dust settles and becomes gritty between the teeth, and down the back of the neck, and inside the shoes, where it is discovered to have produced blisters.

Gilvan and Alora led their new-found friends and relatives, and their reclaimed daughter and her young man, and the now-exhausted escort of twenty, dripping flowers, and those from beyond the border who had followed their King and Queen, into the palace gardens, and shut the door firmly behind them. The people outside still cheered, but it was observed that the crowds broke up fairly quickly, and rushed around to the front of the palace, where they might expect a speech from the Balcony of Public Appearances and Addresses that would explain everything to them. They did not have to wait long; Gilvan motioned aside the ladies-and-gentlemen-in-waiting—and all the fascinated onlookers who had arranged themselves in the halls and courtyards—and said, "It's hardly fair to make them out there wait for their wash and brushup while we have ours—but for heaven's sake go stir up the kitchen, we're as hungry as bears."

It was Alora who did the introducing, as the six of them stood on the balcony and strained their eyes to see the end of the crowd, and as the members of the crowd jostled for position and strained their eyes to see the six on the balcony. "This is my sister, Ellian, whom we have not seen for so many long years; she is now Queen Ellian, consort of King Thold, and they rule together that country next to ours"—here there was a pause, but it could be explained that Alora was shouting as loudly as she could and at this point needed a deep breath—"the Land Beyond the Trees."

Everybody cheered, and nobody minded, even those who knew what was going on, and those too far away to hear, who tried to wait patiently till they could tackle someone who had secured a better position and could tell them what had been said.

Then Linadel and Donathor were brought forward, and Gilvan announced, "And this is Prince Donathor, eldest son of King Thold and Queen Ellian, and the betrothed of our daughter, the Princess Linadel: and the wedding will be celebrated in a fortnight's time."

Everybody cheered again, but hushed very quickly as Queen Ellian stepped forward: and some of those who recognized her from her youth found their eyes growing dim as they saw how much lovelier she had become.

"And we have all agreed that we are proud and happy that our children should reign jointly over our two kingdoms after we retire, and the celebration of this wedding will also be a celebration of the unity of our two countries in a new understanding and fellowship. For too long our two countries have turned their faces from each other, as if they were separate planets and the air each breathed was inimical to the other. Henceforward we shall be neighbors, good neighbors and friends, in all things."

And this time the cheering went on for so very long that people did begin to feel hoarse, and then everybody went home for dinner, and Alora, Gilvan, Ellian, Thold, Linadel, and Donathor were very glad to descend from the balcony to the baths and dinner awaiting them.

EPILOGUE

THE TWO WEEKS passed, and the wedding was performed, and everyone from both sides of the border came to Alora's and Gilvan's palace for the ceremony, and stayed for the week's feasting after; and all were happy. But, of course, it did not end there.

The door in the hedge had remained open for those two weeks of preparation; for Ellian, having recovered her sister, would not let her go; nor would Alora think of parting with her. And then too the parents of the betrothed pair had many things to plan and discuss together; and they found not only that they could work cheerfully together, but that they were friends almost at once; not only the two sisters, but also the two Kings. Within a few days so many old wounds had healed over that Gilvan remembered how Ellian had teased him, long ago, about being besotted with her sister, while Ellian herself had managed to remain free of such entanglements. Gilvan reminded her of it, and she laughed, and teased him all over again, saying that the years hadn't changed him in the least, and that furthermore she was glad of it.

Perhaps they did not think of what that open door in the hedge would bring about, or perhaps they put it deliberately out of their minds, or perhaps they recognized that the time of choice had passed with the end of that first meeting in the strange forest, where briefly they had stood on ground that existed as two places at once; and so they resigned themselves to the inevitable. If any of the mortals had any consciousness of what was happening, beyond anyone's power now to halt, it was Gilvan; for Alora was too caught up in the tumultuous delight of having not only a daughter, but an excellent husband for that daughter, and a sister besides.

It was Gilvan who woke up one night and found himself thinking before he was awake enough to realize where his thoughts were taking him and deflect them in time. And his thoughts said to him: "When was the time of choice? When did you stand at the crossroads and say this way— not that? Could any of us, in that uncanny wood, have said, 'No—I condemn my child to eternal wandering—I know for certain what will come of it else, and know for certain that it would be evil'?" He lay staring at the starlight, turning his life, and his wife's, and his daughter's, over in his mind as best he could; and then, because he was a king, he considered the lives of his country and his people; and at the end he could still only reply, "I don't know."

He turned to look at Alora and, as if even in her sleep she sensed some anxiety in her husband, she crept nearer him and laid her head on his shoulder. Perhaps it was the rosy smile on her lips that cured him, but eventually he fell asleep again.

For while the door in the hedge remained open, any could pass through, again and again if they chose, and for any reason; for the door was now always there, near the tree with the yellow fruit, and the thin stream broken by rocks that no longer moved in their places. And the mothers and fathers of long-lost infants, and the forlorn sweethearts of young ladies who had disappeared behind that hedge, went through that door: and many found what they sought. No mortal can remain unchanged after meeting again with a loved one who has been touched by the faeries; and the change is all the more profound for its being little realized. There were some, too, from the far side of the border who came to the near side, to seek what they had lost: for it is only purblind mortals who suppose that they have a monopoly on bereavement. But it was a lesson to the immortals that creatures of so short a life span can sincerely grieve: for only immortals can disregard time.

And so families met again, faerie as well as human; and too much knowledge exchanged hands, though little of it was spoken aloud. No mortal should understand why the babies stolen are always boys, while the girls who are taken have first gained some number of years; no faerie should comprehend what can call a fellow immortal back over the border, once crossed by one originally human, who became a grandmother or grandfather of immortals, and yet passed on some almost mortal restlessness to their descendants. None should: but some ties are too strong for such division, and the families spoke blood to blood, and the lovers heart to heart, and understanding came, and with it, change.

So it was that even after the first fortnight, during the wedding, and the brilliant, giddy, overfed week that followed it, Gilvan could smell a change in the air, a tone in the pitch of the people's cheers that was different from that which had first rung over the heads of the returning Linadel and her Donathor. If he had been willing to face this sense of change squarely, he could have argued with himself that this was because there were as many faeries present for the celebration as there were of his own people, and they had perhaps different-sounding lungs. But since he did not face it squarely, he did not have to argue speciously with himself, and he was left with the accurate if unspecific sense that something—something—had shifted.

Later he caught that same knowledge looking out of Alora's eyes; but as soon as each recognized it in the other, each swiftly drew a curtain over it, and they smiled at one another, and raised their wine goblets in a toast that neither uttered but both most sincerely meant.

As Alora and Gilvan knew it quickly, it being their own country, and they as sensitive to everything that moved within it as young birds are to the changing seasons, so Thold and at last Ellian—for she knew both countries too well and neither well enough—knew it too. At first, for them, it was but a suspicion, guarded and held by the same knowledge behind that meeting in the wood that woke Gilvan up at night; but they knew it themselves beyond doubt when the wedding party came back to the Land Beyond the Trees for a second celebration, and for friends to see how each other lived.

The change was never discussed. There was no need and no purpose for it. Linadel and Donathor learned it in their turn, not as their parents had, by a change in their two peoples, but by the growing apprehension, as they traveled back and forth from the land of Linadel's birth to that of Donathor's, that the two peoples they had thought they were to rule were not any more to be differentiated. They had become one, as their next King and Queen had before them.

The first faerie-to-mortal marriage that came from the door in the hedge was that of one of the girls who had held the golden ribbons for Linadel. She had dropped the shining ribbon when the beautiful mortal Princess had turned away, and she had wept with her Queen when Donathor and Linadel chose to lose everything rather than each other; and she had followed Ellian and Thold when they followed their son and his bride. And during that meeting in the woods, this golden girl had met one of the courtiers who for love of his own King and Queen had followed them on their despairing journey in search of their daughter. And when these two were married, they asked that the royal blessing that every marriage on either side of the border had always been granted be given by Linadel and Donathor; for they were the living symbol of all that had happened and was happening. And that first marriage was a symbol too: of the love the new changed people had for their new King and Queen.

To her considerable embarrassment, and the great delight of everybody else (especially Gilvan), ten months after her daughter's wedding, Alora gave birth to a son;

and they named him Senan. He grew up green-eyed and musical, and cared very little that he was a prince, for he preferred to tie his harp to his back and wander far over the hills and through the forests of all the lands within reach of his tireless walking; and there were none that were not within reach. Each time he returned to the land of his birth, he sang songs to his family and his people of the wonders he had seen; but no one was ever sure if he had seen them as other people saw, or if it was the music that did the seeing; for no one doubted that he and his harp could speak to each other as one friend to another; and all had heard his laughing claim that there were no bones in his body, only tunes, and no blood, but poetry.

The door in the hedge became many doors, and Alora's and Gilvan's kingdom became almost one more vast meadow within the wide pattern of the hedges and trees of Faerieland; for as the border dissolved on one side, a new border began to grow up opposite. Fewer people came from outside to settle in that last mortal kingdom as it became less and less a last mortal kingdom; and even fewer left it to seek their fortunes elsewhere, because the look that Gilvan had first seen in Donathor's eyes had soon settled in his own, and in those of his people. There it rooted deep.

In the end the new border grew up, wild and thick and full of thorns; for one thing that the once-mortals and the immortals had learned of each other was the heartbreak they had once each caused the other; and when their ignorance had passed, it seemed that their restlessness passed too, and from this they concluded that they could venture no further with neighbors beyond the new border.

But none knew either where Senan went, for he went wherever he chose; the borders were nothing to him.

When it came time for Gilvan and Alora to retire—they having remained long enough to gloat over two granddaughters and two grandsons—Thold and Ellian decided to retire at the same time, and the four of them went together into the mountains Ellian had spoken to Linadel about at their first meeting; and where the sisters' parents—who were no longer stout or stuffy, and looked like the finest blooms in their own garden—and much faerie majesty were there and waiting for them.

Linadel and Donathor ruled over a happy land, a wiser one than it is the fortune of most sovereigns to rule, and one of a breadth and scope that none could quite measure; and they had several more children, and convinced their respective parents to visit them somewhat more often than had been the tradition for retired majesty. Everyone was contented and some restless few were great, and tales were told of their deeds; but, except for Senan's music, by the time that Linadel and Donathor had in their turn retired, there was no more communication with the rest of the world.

So it has been now for many long generations, more than anyone can name, for the tale has been passed from mouth to mouth too often. But the world turns, and even legends change; and somewhere there is a border, and sometime, perhaps, someone will decide to cross it, however well guarded with thorns it may be.

The Princess and the Frog

PART ONE

SHE HELD the pale necklace in her hand and stared at it as she walked. Her feet evidently knew where they were going, for they did not stumble although her eyes gave them no guidance. Her eyes remained fixed on the glowing round stones in her hand.

These stones were as smooth as pearls, and their color, at first sight, seemed as pure. But they were much larger than any pearls she had ever seen; as large as the dark sweet cherries she plucked in the palace gardens. And their pale creamy color did not lie quiet and reflect the sunlight, but shimmered and shifted, and seemed to offer her glimpses of something mysterious in their hearts, something she waited to see, almost with dread, which was always at the last minute hidden from her. And they seemed to have a heat of their own that owed nothing to her hand as she held them; rather they burned against her cold fingers. Her hand trembled, and their cloudy swirling seemed to shiver in response; the swiftness of their ebb and flow seemed to mock the pounding of her heart.

Prince Aliyander had just given her the necklace, with one of the dark-eyed smiles she had learned to fear so much; for while he had done nothing to her yet—but then, he had *done* nothing to any of them—she knew that her own brother was under his invisible spell. This spell he called "friendship" with his flashing smile and another look from his black eyes; and her own father, the King, was afraid of him. She also knew he meant to marry her, and knew her strength could not hold out against him long, once he set himself to win her. His "friendship" had already subdued the Crown Prince, only a few months ago a merry and mischievous lad, into a dog to follow at his heels and go where he was told.

This morning, as they stood together in the Great Hall, herself, and her father, and Prince Aliyander, with the young Crown Prince a half-step behind Aliyander's right shoulder, and their courtiers around them, Aliyander had reached into a pocket and brought out the neckace. It gleamed and seemed to shiver with life as he held it up, and all the courtiers murmured with awe. "For you, Lady Princess," said Aliyander, with a graceful bow and his smile; and he moved to fasten it around her neck: "a small gift, to tell you of just the smallest portion of my esteem for Your Highness."

She started back with a suddenness that surprised even her; and her heart flew up in her throat and beat there wildly as the great jewels danced before her eyes. And she felt rather than saw the flicker in Aliyander's eyes when she moved away from him.

"Forgive me," she stammered; "they are so lovely, you must let me look at them a little first." Her voice felt thick; it was hard to speak. "I shan't be able to admire them as they deserve, when they lie beneath my chin."

"Of course," said Aliyander, but she could not look at his smile. "All pretty ladies love to look at pretty things"; and the edge in his voice was such that only she felt it; and she had to look away from the Crown Prince, whose eyes were shining with the delight of his friend's generosity.

"May I—may I take your—gracious gift outside, and look at it in the sunlight?" she faltered. The high vaulted ceiling and mullioned windows seemed suddenly narrow and stifling, with the great glowing stones only inches from her face. The touch of sunlight would be healing. She reached out blindly, and tried not to wince as Aliyander laid the necklace across her hand.

"I hope you will return wearing my poor gift," he said, with the same edge to his words, "so that it may flatter itself in the light of Your Highness's beauty, and bring joy to the heart of your unworthy admirer."

"Yes—yes, I will," she said, and turned, and only her Princess's training prevented her from fleeing, picking up her skirts with her free hand and running the long length of the Hall to the arched doors, and outside to the gardens. Or perhaps it was the imponderable weight in her hand that held her down.

But outside, at least the sky did not shut down on her as the walls and groined ceiling of the Hall had; and the sun seemed to lie gently and sympathetically across her shoulders even if it could not help itself against Aliyander's jewels, and dripped and ran across them until her eyes were dazzled.

Her feet stopped at last, and she blinked and looked up. Near the edge of the garden, near the great outer wall of the palace, was a quiet pool with a few trees close around it, so that much of the water stood in shadow wherever the sun stood in the sky. There was a small white marble bench under one of the trees, pushed close enough that a sitter might lean comfortably against the broad bole behind him. Aside from the bench there was no other ornament; as the palace gardens went, it was almost wild, for the grass was allowed to grow a little shaggy before it was cut back, and wildflowers grew here occasionally, and were undisturbed. The Princess had discovered this spot—for no one else seemed to come here but the occasional gardener and his clippers—about a year ago; a little before Prince Aliyander had ridden into their lives. Since that riding, their lives had changed, and she had come here more and more often, to be quiet and alone, if only for a little time.

Now she stood at the brink of the pond, the strange necklace clutched in her unwilling fingers, and closed her eyes. She took a few long breaths, hoping that the cool peacefulness of this place would somehow help even this trouble. She did not want to wear this necklace, to place it around her throat; she felt that the strange jewels would . . . strangle her, stop her breath . . . till she breathed in the same rhythm as Aliyander, and as her poor brother.

Her trembling stopped; the hand with the necklace dropped a few inches. She felt better. But as soon as she opened her eyes, she would see those terrible cloudy stones again. She raised her chin. At least the first thing she would see was the quiet water. She began to open her eyes: and then a great *croak* bellowed from, it seemed, a place just beside her feet; and her overtaxed nerves broke out in a sharp "Oh," and she leaped away from the sound. As she leaped, her fingers opened, and the necklace dropped with the softest splash, a lingering and caressing sound, and disappeared under the water.

Her first thought was relief that the stones no longer held and threatened her; and then she remembered Aliyander, and her heart shrank within her. She remembered his look when she had refused his gift; and the sound of his voice when he hoped she would wear it upon her return to the Hall—where he was even now awaiting her. She dared not face him without it round her neck; and he would never believe in this accident. And, indeed, if she had cared for the thing, she would have pulled it to her instead of loosing it in her alarm.

She knelt at the edge of the pool and looked in; but while the water seemed clear, and the sunlight penetrated a long way, still she could not see the bottom, but only a misty greyness that drowned at last to utter black. "Oh dear," she whispered. "I *must* get it back. But how?"

"Well," said a voice diffidently, "I think I could probably fetch it for you."

She had forgotten the noise that had startled her. The voice came from very low down; she was kneeling with her hands so near the pool's edge that her fingertips were lightly brushed by the water's smallest ripples. She turned her head and looked down still farther; and sitting on the bank at her side she saw one of the largest frogs she had ever seen. She did not even think to be startled. "It was rather my fault anyway," added the frog.

"Oh—could you?" she said. She hardly thought of the phenomenon of a frog that talked; her mind was taken up with wishing to have the necklace back, and reluctance to see and touch it again. Here was one part of her problem solved; the medium of the solution did not matter to her.

The frog said no more, but dived into the water with scarcely more noise than the necklace had made in falling; in what seemed only a moment its green head emerged again, with two of the round stones in its wide mouth. It clambered back onto the bank, getting entangled in the trailing necklace as it did so. A frog is a silly creature, and this one looked absurd, with a king's ransom of smooth heavy jewels twisted round its squat figure; but she did not think of this. She reached out to help, and it wasn't till she had Aliyander's gift in her hands again that she noticed the change.

The stones were as large and round and perfect as they had been before; but the weird creamy light of them was gone. They lay dim and grey and quiet against her palm, as cool as the water of the pond, and strengthless.

Such was her relief and pleasure that she sprang to her feet, spreading the necklace to its fullest extent and turning it this way and that in the sunlight, to be certain of what she saw; and she forgot even to thank the frog, still sitting patiently on the bank where she had rescued it from the binding necklace.

"Excuse me," it said at last, and then she remembered it, and looked down and said, "Oh, thank you," with such a bright and glowing look that it might move even a frog's cold heart.

"You're quite welcome, I'm sure," said the frog mechanically. "But I wonder if I might ask you a favor."

"Certainly. Anything." Even facing Aliyander seemed less dreadful, now the necklace was quenched: she felt that perhaps he could be resisted. Her joy made her silly; it was the first time anything of Aliyander's making had missed its mark, and for a moment she had no thoughts for the struggle ahead, but only for the present victory. Perhaps even the Crown Prince could be saved. . . .

"Would you let me live with you at the palace for a little time?"

Her wild thoughts halted for a moment, and she looked down bewildered at the frog. What would a frog want with a palace? For that matter—as if she had only just noticed it—why did this frog talk?

"I find this pool rather dull," said the frog fastidiously, as if this were an explanation.

She hesitated, dropping her hands again, but this time the stones hung limply, hiding in a fold of her wide skirts. She had told the frog, "Certainly, anything"; and her father had brought her up to understand that she must always keep her word, the more so because as Princess there was no one who could force her to. "Very well," she said at last. "If you wish it." And she realized after she spoke that part of her hesitation was reluctance that anything, even a frog, should see her palace, her family, now; it would hurt her. But she had given her word, and there could be no harm in a frog.

"Thank you," said the frog gravely, and with surprising dignity for a small green thing with long thin flipper-footed legs and popping eyes.

There was a pause, and then she said, "I—er—I think I should go back now. Will you be along later or—?"

"I'll be along later," replied the frog at once, as if he recognized her embarrassment; as if he were a poor relation who yet had a sense of his own worth.

She hesitated a moment longer, wondering to how many people she would have to explain her talking frog, and added, "I dine alone with my father at eight." Prince Inthur never took his meals with his father and sister any more; he ate with Aliyander or alone, miserably, in his room, if Aliyander chose to overlook him. Then she raised the grey necklace to clasp it round her throat, and remembered that it was, after all, her talking frog's pool that had put out the ill light of Aliyander's work. She smiled once more at the frog, a little guiltily, for she believed one should be kind to one's poor relations; and she said, "You'll be my talisman."

She turned and walked quickly away, back toward the palace, and the Hall, and Aliyander.

PART TWO

BUT SHE MADE a serious mistake, for she walked swiftly back to the Hall, and blithely through the door, with her head up and her eyes sparkling with happiness and release; she met Aliyander's black eyes too quickly, and smiled without thinking. It was only then she realized what her thoughtlessness had done, when she saw his eyes move swiftly from her face to the jewels at her throat, and then as he saw her smile his own face twisted with a rage so intense it seemed for a moment that his sallow skin would turn black with it. And even her little brother, the Crown Prince, looked at his hero a little strangely, and said, "Is anything wrong?"

Aliyander did not answer. He turned on his heel and left, going toward the door opposite that which the Princess had entered; the door that led into the rest of the palace. Everyone seemed to be holding his or her breath while the quiet footfalls retreated, for there was no other noise; even the air had stopped moving through the windows. Then there was the sound of the heavy door opening, and closing, and Aliyander was gone.

The courtiers blinked and looked at one another. The Crown Prince looked as if he might cry: his master had left him behind. The King turned to his daughter with the closing of that far door, and he saw first her white frightened face; and then his gaze dropped to the round stones of her necklace, and there, for several moments, it remained.

No one of the courtiers looked at her directly; but when she caught their sidelong looks, there was blankness in their eyes, not understanding. None addressed a word to her, although all had seen that she, somehow, was the cause of Aliyander's anger. But then, for months now it had been considered bad luck to discuss anything that Aliyander did.

Inthur, the Crown Prince, still loved his father and sister in spite of the cloud that Aliyander had cast over his mind; and little did he know how awkward Aliyander found that simple and indestructible love. But now Inthur saw his sister standing alone in the doorway to the garden, her face as white as her dress, and as a little gust of wind blew her skirts around her, and her fair hair across her face, she gasped and gave a shudder, and one hand touched her necklace. With Aliyander absent, even the cloud on Inthur lifted a little, although he himself did not know this, for he never thought about himself. Instead he ran the several steps to where his sister stood, and threw his arms around her; he looked up into her face and said, "Don't worry, Rana dear, he's never angry long." His boy's gaze passed over the necklace without a pause.

She nodded down at him and tried to smile, but her eyes filled with tears; and with a little brother's horror of tears, particularly sister's tears, he let go of her at once and said quickly, with the air of one who changes the subject from one proved dangerous, "What did you do?"

She blinked back her tears, recognizing the dismay on Inthur's face; he would not know that it was his hug that had brought them, and the look on his face when he tried to comfort her: just as he had used to look before Aliyander came. Now he rarely glanced at either his father or his sister except vaguely, as if half asleep, or with his thoughts far away. "I don't know," she said, with a fair attempt at calmness, "but perhaps it is not important."

He patted her hand as if he were her uncle, and said, "That's all right. You just apologize to him when you see him next, and it'll be over."

She smiled wanly as she remembered that her own brother belonged to Aliyander now and she could not trust him. Then the King came up beside them, and when her eyes met his she read knowledge in them: of what Aliyander had seen, in her face and round her neck; and a reflection of her own fear. He said nothing to her.

The rest of the day passed slowly, for while they did not see Aliyander again, the weight of his absence was almost as great as his presence would have been. The Crown Prince grew cross and fretful, and glowered at everyone; the courtiers seemed nervous, and whispered among themselves, looking often over their shoulders as if for the ghosts of their great-grandmothers. Even those who came from the city, or the far-flung towns beyond, to kneel before the King and crave a favor seemed more to crouch and plead, as if for mercy; and their faces were never happy when they went away, whatever the King had granted them.

Rana felt as grey as Aliyander's jewels.

The sun set at last, and its final rays touched the faces in the Hall with the first color most of them had had all day; and as servants came in to light the candles everyone looked paler and more uncomfortable than ever.

One of Aliyander's personal servants approached the throne soon after the candles were lit; the King sat with his children in smaller chairs at his feet. The man offered the Crown Prince a folded slip of paper; his obeisance to the King first was a gesture so cursory as to be insulting, but the King made no move to reprimand him. The Hall was as still as it had been that morning when Aliyander had left it; and the sound of Inthur's impatient opening of the note crackled loudly. He leaped to his feet and said joyfully, "I'm to dine with him!" and with a dreadful look of triumph round the Hall, and then at his father and sister—Rana closed her eyes—he ran off, the servant following with the dignity of a nobleman.

It seemed a sign. The King stood up wearily and clapped his hands once; and the courtiers made their bows and began to drift away, to quarters in the palace, or to grand houses outside in the city. Rana followed her father to the door that led to the rest of the palace, where the Crown Prince had just disappeared; and there the King turned and said, "I will see you at eight, my child?" And Rana's eyes again filled with tears at the question in his voice, behind his words. She only nodded, afraid to speak, and he turned away. "We dine alone," he said, and left her.

She spent two long and bitter hours staring at nothing, sitting alone in her room; in spite of the gold-and-white hangings, and the bright blue coverlet on her bed, it refused to look cheerful for her tonight. She removed her necklace and stuffed it into an empty jar and put the lid on quickly, as if it were a snake that might escape, although she knew that it itself had no further power to harm her.

She joined her father with a heavy heart; in place of Aliyander's jewels she wore a golden pendant that her mother had given her. The two of them ate in a little room with a small round table, where her family had always gathered when there was no formal banquet. When she was very small, and Inthur only a baby, she had sat here with both her parents; then her pretty, fragile mother had died, and she and Inthur and their father had faced each other around this table alone. Now it was just the King and herself. There had been few banquets in the last months. As she looked at her father now, she was suddenly frightened at how old and weak he looked. Aliyander could gain no hold over him, for his mind and his will were too pure for Aliyander's nets; but his presence aged him quickly, too quickly. And the next King would be Inthur, who followed Aliyander everywhere, a pace behind his right shoulder. And Inthur would be delighted at his best friend's marrying his sister.

The dining-room was round like the table within it; it

was the first floor of a tower that stood at one of the many corners of the Palace. It had windows on two sides, and a door through which the servants brought the covered dishes and the wine, and another door that led down a flight of stone steps to the garden.

Neither she nor her father ate much, nor spoke at all, and the room was very quiet. So it was that when an odd muffled thump struck the garden door, they both looked up at once. Whatever it was, after a moment it struck again. They stared at each other, puzzled, and because since Aliyander had come all things unknown were dreaded, their looks were also fearful. When the third thump came, Rana stood up and went over to the door and flung it open.

There sat her frog.

"Oh!" she exclaimed. "It's you."

If a frog could turn its foolish mouth to a smile, this one did. "Good evening," it replied.

"Who is it?" said the King, standing up; for he could see nothing, yet he heard the strange deep voice.

"It's . . . a frog," Rana said, somewhat embarrassed. "I dropped . . . that necklace in a pool today, and he fetched it out for me. He asked a favor in return, that he might live with me in the palace."

"If you made a promise, child, you must keep it," said the King; and for a moment he looked as he had before Aliyander came. "Invite him in." And his eyes rested on his daughter thoughtfully, remembering the change in those jewels that he had seen.

The Princess stood aside, and the frog hopped in. The King and Princess stood, feeling silly, looking down, while the frog looked up; then Rana shook herself, and shut the door, and returned to the table. "Would you—er—like some dinner? There's plenty."

She took the frog back to her own room in her pocket. Her father had said nothing to her about their odd visitor, but she knew from the look on his face when he bade her good night that he would mention it to no one. The frog said gravely that her room was a very handsome one; then it leaped up onto a sofa and settled itself among the cushions. Rana blew the lights out and undressed and climbed into bed, and lay, staring up, thinking.

"I will go with you to the Hall tomorrow, if I may," said the frog's voice from the darkness, breaking in on her dark thoughts.

"Certainly," she said, as she had said once before. "You're my talisman," she added, with a catch in her voice.

"All is not well here," said the frog gently; and the deep sympathetic voice might have been anyone, not a frog, but her old nurse, perhaps, when she was a baby and needed comforting because of a scratched knee; or the best friend she had never had, because she was a Princess, the only Princess of the greatest realm in all the lands from the western to the eastern seas; and to her horror, she burst into tears and found herself between gulps telling that voice everything. How Aliyander had ridden up one day, without warning, ridden in from the north, where his father still ruled as king over a country bordering her father's. How Aliyander was now declared the heir apparent, for his elder brother, Lian, had disappeared over a year before; and while this sad loss continued mysteriously, still it was necessary for the peace of the country to secure the succession. Aliyander's first official performance as heir apparent was this visit to his kingdom's nearest neighbor to the south, for he knew that it was his father's dearest wish that the friendship between their two lands continue close and loyal.

And for the first time they saw Aliyander smile. The Crown Prince had turned away, for he was then free and innocent; the King stiffened and grew pale; and Rana did not guess how she might have looked.

"I had known Lian when we were children," Rana continued; she no longer cared who was listening, or if anything was. "He was kind and patient with Inthur, who was only a baby; I—I thought him wonderful," she whispered. "I heard my parents discussing him one night, him and . . . me. . . ."

Aliyander's visit had lengthened—a fortnight, a month, two months; it had been almost a year since he rode through their gates. Messengers passed between him and his father—he said; but here he stayed, and entrapped the Crown Prince; and next he would have the Princess.

"I don't know what to do," she said at last, wearily. "There is nothing I can do."

"I'm sorry," said the voice, and it was sad, and wistful, and kind.

And human. Her mind wavered from the single thought of *Aliyander, Aliyander,* and she remembered to whom—or what—she spoke; and the sympathy in the creature's voice puzzled her even more than the fact that the voice could use human speech.

"You cannot be a frog," she said stupidly. "You must

be—under a spell." And she found she could spare a little pity from her own family's plight to give to this spell-bound creature who spoke like a human being.

"Of course," snapped the frog. "Frogs don't talk."

She was silent, sorry that her own pain had made her thoughtless, made her wound another's feelings.

"I'm sorry," said the frog for the second time, and in the same gentle tone. "You see, one never quite grows accustomed."

She answered after a moment: "Yes. I think I do understand, a little."

"Thank you," said the frog.

"Yes," she said again. "Good night."

"Good night."

But just before she fell asleep, she heard the voice once more: "I have one more favor to ask. That you do not mention, when you take me to the Hall tomorrow, that I . . . talk."

"Very well," she said drowsily.

PART THREE

THERE WAS A ripple of nervous laughter when the Princess Rana appeared in the Great Hall on the next morning, carrying a large frog. She held her right arm bent at the elbow and curled lightly against her side; and the frog rode quietly on her forearm. She was wearing a dress of pale blue, with lace at her neck, and her fair hair hung loose over her shoulders, and a silver circlet was around her brow; the big green frog showed brilliantly and absurdly against her pale loveliness. She sat on her low chair before her father's throne; the frog climbed, or slithered, or leaped, to her lap, and lay, blinking foolishly at the noblemen in their rich dresses, and the palace servants in their handsome livery; but it was perhaps too stupid to be frightened, for it made no other motion.

She had seen Aliyander standing with the Crown Prince when she entered, but she avoided his eyes; at last he came to stand before her, legs apart, staring down at her bent head with a heat from his black eyes that scorched her skin.

"You dare to mock me," he said, his voice almost a

hiss, thick with a venomous hatred she could not mistake.

She looked up in terror, and he gestured at the frog. "Ah, no, I meant no—" she pleaded, and then her voice died; but the heat of Aliyander's look ebbed a little as he read the fear in her face.

"A frog, Princess?" he said; his voice still hurt her, but now it was heavy with scorn, and pitched so that many in the Hall would hear him. "I thought Princesses preferred kittens, or greyhounds."

"I—" She paused, and licked her dry lips. "I found it in the garden." She dropped her eyes again; she could think of nothing else to say. If only he would turn away from her—just for a minute, a minute to gather her wits; but he would not leave her, and her wits would only scatter again when next he addressed her.

He made now a gesture of disgust; and then straightened up, as if he would turn away from her at last, and she clenched her hands on the arms of her chair —and at that moment the frog gave its great bellow, the noise that had startled her yesterday into dropping the necklace into the pool. And Aliyander was startled; he jerked visibly—and the courtiers laughed.

It was only the barest titter, and strangled instantly; but Aliyander heard it, and he turned, his face black with rage as it had been yesterday when Rana had returned wearing a cold grey necklace; and he seized the frog by the leg and hurled it against the heavy stone wall opposite the thrones, which stood halfway down the long length of the Hall and faced across the narrow width to tall windows that looked out upon the courtyard.

Rana was frozen with horror for the moment it took

Aliyander to fling the creature; and then as it struck the wall, there was a dreadful sound, and the skin of the frog seemed to—burst—and she closed her eyes.

The sudden gasp of all those around her made her eyes open against her will. And she in her turn gasped.

For the frog that Aliyander had hurled against the wall was there no longer; as it struck and fell, it became a tall young man, who stood there now, his ruddy hair falling past his broad shoulders, his blue eyes blazing as he stared at his attacker.

"Aliyander," he said, and his voice fell like a stone in the silence. Aliyander stood as if his name on those lips had turned him to stone indeed.

"Aliyander. My little brother."

No one moved but Rana; her hands stirred of their own accord. They crept across the spot on her lap where the frog had lain only a minute ago; and they seized each other.

Aliyander laughed—a terrible, ugly sound. "I defeated you once, big brother. I will defeat you again. You are weaker than I. You always will be."

The blue eyes never wavered. "Yes, I am weaker," Lian replied, "as you have proven already. I do not choose your sort of power."

Aliyander's face twisted as Rana had seen it before. She stood up suddenly, but he paid no attention to her; the heat of his gaze was now reserved for his brother, who stood calmly enough, staring back at Aliyander's distorted face.

"You made the wrong choice," Aliyander said, in a voice as black as his look; "and I will prove it to you.

You will have no chance to return and inconvenience me a second time."

It was as if no one else could move; the eyes of all were riveted on the two antagonists; even the Crown Prince did not move to be closer to his hero.

The Princess turned and ran. She paused on the threshold of the door to the garden, and picked up a tall flagon that had held wine and was now sitting forgotten on a deep windowsill. Then she ran out, down the white paths; she had no eyes for the trees and the flowers, or the smooth sand of the courtyard to her right; she felt as numb as she had the day before with her handful of round and glowing jewels; but today her eyes watched where her feet led her, and her mind said *hurry, hurry, hurry.*

She ran to the pond where she had found the frog, or where the frog had found her. She knelt quickly on the bank, and rinsed the sour wine dregs from the bottom of the flagon she carried, emptying the tainted water on the grass behind her, where it would not run back into the pool. Then she dipped the jug full, and carried it, brimming, back to the Great Hall.

She had to walk slowly this time, for the flagon was full and very heavy, and she did not wish to spill even a drop of it. Her feet seemed to sink ankle-deep in the ground with every step, although in fact the white pebbles held no footprint as she passed, and only bruised her small feet in their thin-soled slippers.

She paused on the Hall's threshold again, this time for her eyes to adjust to the dimmer light. No one had moved; and no one looked at her.

She saw Aliyander raise his hand and bring it like a back-handed slap against the air before him; and though Lian stood across the room from him, she saw his head jerk as if from the force of a blow; and a thin line formed on his cheek, and after a moment blood welled and dripped from it.

Aliyander waved his hand so the sharp stone of his ring glittered; and he laughed.

Rana started forward again, step by step, as slowly as she had paced the garden, although only a few steps more were needed. Her arms had begun to shiver with the weight of her burden. Still Aliyander did not look at her; for while his might be the greater strength at last, still he could not tear his eyes away from the calm clear gaze of his brother's; his brother yet held him.

Rana walked up the narrow way till she was so close to Aliyander that she might have touched his sleeve if she had not needed both hands to hold the flagon. Then, at last, Aliyander broke away to look at her; and as he did she lifted the great jug, and with a strength she thought was not hers alone, hurled the contents full upon the man before her.

He gave a strangled cry, and· brushed desperately with his hands as if he could sweep the water away; but he was drenched with it, his hair plastered to his head and his clothes to his body. He looked suddenly small, wizened and old. He still looked at her, but she met his gaze fearlessly, and he did not seem to recognize her.

His face turned as grey as his jewels. His eyes, she thought, were as opaque as the eyes of marble statues; and then he fell down full-length upon the floor, heavily, without sound, with no attempt to catch himself. He moved no more.

Inthur leaped up then with a cry, and ran to his fallen friend, and Rana saw the quick tears on his cheeks; but when he looked up he looked straight at her, and his eyes were clear. "He was my friend," he said simply; but there was no memory in him of what that friendship had been.

The King stood down stiffly from his throne, and the courtiers moved, and shook themselves as if from sleep, and stared without sorrow at the still body of Aliyander, and with curiosity and awe and a little hesitant but hopeful joy at Lian.

"I welcome you," said the King, with the pride of the master of his own hall, and of a king of a long line of kings. "I welcome you, Prince Lian, to my country, and to my people." And his gaze flickered only briefly to the thing on the floor; at his gesture, a servant stepped forward and threw a dark cloth over it.

"Thank you," said Lian gravely; and the Princess realized that he had come up silently and was standing at her side. She glanced up and saw him looking down at her; and the knowledge of what they had done together, and what neither could have done alone, passed between them; and with it an understanding that they would never discuss it. She said aloud: "I—I welcome you, Prince Lian."

"Thank you," he said again, but she heard the change of tone in his voice; and from the corner of her eye she saw her father smile. She offered Lian her hand, and he took it, and raised it slowly to his lips.

The
Hunting
of the
Hind

PART ONE

THE HUNTS continued as they always had, for the game they killed was necessary for food; but there was no joy in them now, and few people attended, or rode with the Master, except those who must. There could be no pleasure in the chase while the King's only and much beloved son lay sick on his bed, paler and weaker with every day that passed, and raving always about the Golden Hind.

The Prince had ridden often with the Hunt; his horses were always fine and sleek and proud, and he sat them well; and he himself was as kind as he was handsome, and everyone loved to look at him, and loved more to speak with him. He had a word for everyone, and he remembered every man's name whom he had once met, down to the last village girl-child who gravely presented him with a fresh-picked daisy and her name, wise in all the dignity of her four years of age.

It was but a month gone by that the tragedy had occurred. The sighting of the Golden Hind had troubled the Hunt several times in the past two years; troubled, because the sight of her ruined the dogs, deerhounds tall

and fleet and rabbithounds resolute and sturdy, for the
rest of the day of that sighting. The dogs would not then
follow her, nor any other game, but cowered to the
ground, or ran in circles and howled. Thus it was that all
realized that this Hind, although she was of a color to
bring wonder to the cruelest eyes and tenderness to the
darkest heart, was not a canny thing; and so men feared
her, and feared that sight of her might prove an omen
for more ill than just of that day's hunting.

But as the legend of her grew with the months that
passed, some men saw the following of her as an adventure
by which they might test their courage; and so the boldest
men of the country rode their swiftest horses to join the
Hunt, in the hope of a glimpse of her.

Twelve of them in the space of a year had their wish.
Ten came home again, weary and footsore, and grim with
a depression that seemed to be of something more than
mere exhaustion or failure of a simple chase; their clothes
in tatters and their faces cut by branches and thorns. And
their horses were often lame and more often nervous,
with a thin edge of fear that never again dulled, so that
some of the finest horses in the land could no longer be
ridden trustfully, for they shied and neighed at nothing,
or ran suddenly away with their riders, their dark eyes
white-ringed.

The other two of those twelve men who rode away in
pursuit of the Golden Hind were never seen again, nor
anything heard of their fate.

But a thirteenth joined the Hunt on a day that the
Golden Hind was seen when the Hunt had barely left the
city gates and entered the forest; and the Hunt had to

turn and go back into the city, taking the shaking fearful dogs back to the kennels they had only just left, while the thirteenth man set spurs to his horse, and the Hind fled light-footed away from him.

The thirteenth man returned that evening after sunset, his horse covered with pale foam and a broken rattle in its throat; the rider was mad. They had to drag him out of the saddle, and he fought them, shouting words, if they were words at all, in a language that none could recognize, till they had to bind him, to protect not only themselves but this man from his own madness. Nor did he recognize his wife when they brought him to her; and she wept helplessly for him.

The Prince was a brave man, and as bold as a man confident in his courage might be; and he declared that he would hunt the Hind. But his father forbade him, and when he forbade him, he turned so white that the Prince, who loved his father, reluctantly agreed to obey; for he was capable of going against his father's wishes if his own desires were strong enough. But he continued as before to ride sometimes with the Hunt; and once he rode on a day when one of the twelve men rode too, and they saw the Hind, and the Hunt saw this man ride away in pursuit while the Prince had to remain behind, reining in his high-blooded horse, which was not accustomed to watching another man's horse leap away from him and run alone and unchallenged. The Prince remembered the King's command and his own promise, and he watched only, and then turned his fretful stallion's face toward home. But it did not go down well with him, for he was a proud man as well as a good and kind and brave one, and some of his

horse's restiveness may have been the fault of the rider's
mood.

The thirteenth man was a dear friend of the Prince's.
They had known each other since boyhood, had learned
to ride and to hunt together, and the man's father had
been one of the Prince's father's good friends: the sort of
friend who could speak an unpopular opinion to the King,
and be heard.

The Prince went to visit his old friend and found him
pale and senseless; his black eyes roved without resting,
and he saw nothing that was before him, and started at
shadows that were not there.

The Prince saw that his family lacked for nothing that
a full pocketbook could buy, and returned to his father
with a heavy heart.

"Tomorrow I ride with the Hunt," he told the King.
"And I ride the day after, and the day after that, till I
find what I seek: and that which I seek is the Golden
Hind, and her I will pursue till I learn the mystery of
her, and of the death and madness she causes; and I will
stop these things if I can. Even if I cannot, try at least I
will; my vow is taken." For after he had looked into the
eyes of his friend, that were his friend's eyes no longer,
he did not doubt that the two men who had not returned
from the Hunting of the Hind had on that Hunt met their
deaths. And so the Hind must not be permitted to range
the kingdom, for the proven risk of her.

The King moved to stop him, for he would lose any
number of his people before he would risk his son; but
the Prince left before the King could speak, and no man

saw him again till morning, when he rode out with the Hunt.

It was three days that the Prince rode before he saw what he sought; three days that he spoke to no man and locked himself in his rooms as soon as he dismounted and his horse was led away; three days that he refused to see his father, even when the King himself came and knocked on his son's closed door.

No man saw him to speak to him: but a woman did; or perhaps more rightly, a girl.

The King had married in his youth a woman that he loved, and she loved him, and the country rang with their love; and at the end of several years of hopeful waiting she bore a son. The baby was strong and beautiful; but the Queen had been much weakened by the labor of bearing and birth, and when she bore a second child little more than a year later, it was too much for her unrecovered strength, and she died, and the baby died with her.

The King was shattered by his loss, and the only thing for many months after the Queen's death that could make him smile was his little son, the Prince, who grew more and more like his mother every day; and between the father and son there grew a great love.

But after four years the King yielded to the pleas of his ministers and married again; not because he believed that any child but the beloved son of his first wife would rule after him, but because he could see the usefulness of other sons, to ride at the heads of his armies, and go in state to visit other kingdoms, and be loyal friends (for he could not imagine otherwise) to their eldest brother.

The second Queen was chosen for political compatibility rather than any personal inclination on the part of herself or her new husband. She was as small and dark as the first Queen and the son she had borne were tall and fair; and if this second lady had her own quiet and poignant beauty, few noticed it, for all including the King compared her always with her who had gone before.

But the second Queen carried her part with dignity and without complaint—so far as any knew; and hers was a pale still face at the beginning, so none would notice if it grew paler or stiller.

In one thing was she a disappointment that could be mentioned aloud: she bore no children. At last, in her seventh year as Queen, she became pregnant, and a certain subdued pleasure was visible in the King, who then treated her with a less conscious and more spontaneous kindness than had been his way since she became his wife.

But the child was a girl; and this second Queen too died in childbed, her strength unequal to the effort.

The little Princess grew up, cared for with vague kindness by those around her; the same vague kindness, if she had known it, that had characterized the King's and his country's attitude toward her mother. She, like her half-brother after his, took after her mother: small and quiet, neat in all her motions, and graceful with the unconscious air of a village girl who has never known the attentions of a court. And as she grew she bloomed with her mother's quiet beauty, and perhaps something more that was peculiarly her own; and by the time she reached her seventeenth year, which was the second year since the

Golden Hind had first been sighted in this kingdom, her father's ministers, who had not dared mention marriage again to the King, began to think that the little-valued daughter of the second Queen would make a better political gamepiece than they had anticipated. And, all unconscious of the Hunt and the Hind, they smiled, and began to make plans.

But the Princess knew nothing of these plans. She enjoyed her freedom: That this freedom was the result of the indifference of those who had taken care of her since her mother died she did not notice, or chose not to. She loved her father dutifully, and was always well fed and well dressed, and as she got older, well taught; but there was an unexpected depth to her nature, and she might yet have felt her freedom as sorrow if she had not found someone to love: and the someone was her glorious elder brother.

The Prince was past his eleventh birthday when she was born, but he accepted her at once, and, unlike the rest of the court including his own dearly loved father, the young Prince's acceptance of his little half-sister was sincere and whole-hearted. He called her pet names like "Sparrow" and "Fawn," which suited her and, though she did not realize it, made her mind the less that she was not tall and blond as he himself was. And he not only permitted but encouraged her to follow him around with the unquestioning devotion that most elder brothers find awkward and embarrassing in their younger siblings.

When she grew older, he helped her with her lessons; older yet, and he made sure that her horses were as fine as his own, though lighter-boned to carry her slight weight.

She would have done anything for him; and he, while his love was less single-minded than her own for having more opportunities for loving, cared for her enough that he never took advantage of her; and when she was old enough to understand, he paid her perhaps the highest compliment of all, and made her his friend. The Court noted this, and were perhaps a little more deferential to the little half-sister than they might otherwise have been; and the Princess, by the time she was twelve, knew almost as much about the kingdom as the Prince did, and as much as he could tell her; and by the time she reached her seventeenth year, had a wisdom and discretion far beyond her years.

And so, when the Prince had locked himself away in his rooms and would see no one, the Princess's gentle tap on his door brought him up from his chair to let her in. He told her that he would ride with the Hunt until he saw the Golden Hind; and her he would follow until he learned her secret. He repeated it as if it were a lesson got by heart; and the Princess had already heard the story from several members of the horrified court. She had not doubted it, for she knew the strength of the friendship that had caused her brother to break his promise to the King. Now she wished only to bear him company for a little while; and when she heard the words from his own lips, she only shook her head and said nothing. As she knew her brother, she knew that no argument would sway him.

"Take care of our father till I return," said the Prince; it was the closest he would come to admitting that he might not return. "He loves you better than you know."

The Princess smiled, but shook her head again, for this was one thing she knew better than her elder brother. "I will try." And neither of them spoke of the further grief that made the King's heart desperate at the knowledge of the Prince's vow to follow the Golden Hind: the Prince, although he had passed his eight-and-twentieth birthday, had not yet married. If he died now he would leave no heir. The Princess did not count in the King's thought, as she knew and the Prince did not; so when the Prince commended the King to her care, he thought that he truly left their father some comfort, and did not realize the impossible burden that he laid on his sister's small shoulders.

He rode away with the Hunt the next morning, and returned with them in the evening when they came bearing a brown stag and several hares. He rode away with them on the second dawning, and again on the third; but on that third day, as the sun began to fall down the afternoon sky, the Hunt saw the Golden Hind; and the Prince, with a cry of wild gladness, rode after it. His horse that day was the same tall stallion that had fretted so ill months before, when the Prince had watched another man ride in pursuit of the elusive Hind and had remained behind.

The Hunt came home slowly, but the slinking hounds told their own tale, even if the Prince's shining presence among them had not at once been missed.

The Princess had no sleep that night; nor had the King. But while the King had to rise from his sleepless bed and attend to his state and to his ministers, the Princess remained where she had been since the evening be-

fore, after she had run out to meet the Hunt and foun
her brother no longer with them. She had knelt on th
windowseat of her bedroom all that night, her head lean
ing against the corner where the window met the wall
there she could stare out over the wide dark forest wher
her brother rode after his fate. By the time dawn bega
to chase the shadows out of the castle courtyard, her eye
were sore and her eyelids stiff with watching.

And so the next evening, late, after the Hunt had re
turned that day, sober and slow and with little to sho
for their long hours of search and chase, and after all ha
gone to bed whether they slept or not, the Princess sa
from her window the figure on horseback that stumble
out of the great wood and turned toward the city wall
And there were others keeping watch, so she was not th
first to run out and greet the Prince, for it was he, as h
sat his staggering horse; but she was among the first t
welcome him home. Her voice sounded strange in he
ears, high-pitched with fear, but at the sound of it th
Prince, who seemed to ride in a daze, turned toward he
and said, "Little sister, is it you? Are you there?" Sh
seized his hand joyfully and said, "It is I. You are returne
to us safe."

But when he looked down at her, his eyes did not seer
to see her; and his eyes should have been blue, bu
seemed covered with a grey glaze. "Little sister, I hav
seen her," he said, but he leaned too far over, an
tumbled from his horse into her small young arms; an
if several of the men had not been standing near and s
caught her and him, they would have fallen to th
ground.

The Prince was all but unconscious for the rest of the night; he rambled in his unknown dreams, and spoke snatches of them aloud, but the Princess could not understand, nor could the King, who sat motionless at his son's bedside. With the dawn, some ease came to the Prince, and he did not toss so restlessly, and seemed to sleep. The sun was above the trees when he opened his eyes; and his eyes were blue again. But still he could not seem well to see those around him, and he repeated, "I have seen her at last," again and again. "She is more beautiful than you can imagine," he said, holding his sister's hand in his feverish one. "She could make a man blind with one glimpse of her beauty; and he would count it a favor."

The Prince was too weak to rise from his bed, and grew weaker as the days passed. He recognized his father and sister, and others who came to his bedside, and called them by name; but he could not or would not shake himself free of his dreams, of her whom he had seen, and his blue eyes remained cloudy, and focused only briefly and with evident effort on the faces around him. He slept little and ate less; and the doctors could do nothing for him.

Still the Hunt rode out, because they must; but all feared the sight of the Golden Hind as they might fear Death herself, and no one after the Prince ever sought her.

A month after the Prince rode home from his Hunting of the Hind he was declared to be dying.

The King rarely left his son's room, and his cheeks were almost as pale as the Prince's; the ministers might have run the country as they liked, for all the attention the King paid them; but perhaps almost against their wills they found they loved the bold young Prince too, and their political schemes held no savor.

It might have been that now the little Princess, hitherto neglected for her glamorous elder brother, would come into her own; but this did not happen. Everyone forgot about her completely, except as a small quiet presence forever at the Prince's bedside. Everyone, perhaps, but the Prince himself; for when he asked for anyone, it was most often her name on his lips, and she was always there to answer his call; and she it was who could most often persuade him to take a little food, although even her success was infrequent and insufficient. Again and again he would seize her hand and say to her as he had done on the first night: "I have seen her. At last I have seen her." And his cloudy eyes would be too wide and too brilliant with something she did not recognize and could not help but fear.

The day after the murmur of the Prince dying had passed through the castle and out into the city, the Princess quitted her brother's bedside, where she spent her nights and dozed as she could, just at dawn. She went down to the stable and saddled her favorite horse with her own hands; and when the Hunt gathered, she rode out to join them on her long-legged chestnut mare.

PART TWO

THE HUNT had been quiet enough the last weeks while the Prince lay on his bed and raved; but on the day that the Princess joined them no word at all was spoken, and everyone averted his eyes as if afraid to look upon her, and even the horn-calls to the dogs were subdued. The Princess left no message behind her; but the stablemen would notice the empty stall of the Princess's favorite, as the watchers at her brother's bedside would notice her empty chair.

Morning had barely broken, and the first sunlight had only begun to find its way through the leaves of the forest when the Hunt were brought to a standstill by the long-drawn-out wail of the lead dog. Into a tiny green clearing before them stepped the Golden Hind.

She was a color to make wealthy men weep, and misers drown themselves for very heartsickness. New-minted gold could not express the least shadow of her loveliness; each single hair of her magnificent coat shone with lucent glory. Her delicate hoofs touched the earth without a sound; she turned her small graceful head toward the little group of hunters, seemingly unconscious of the miserable dog that had flattened itself almost at her feet. Her eyes were brown, and for a moment the Princess's eyes met those of this creature of wonder, and it was as though they were only inches from each other in that moment, looking into the depths of each other's souls; for the Princess knew at once that the Hind had a soul, and hope stirred within her. The brown eyes she looked into somewhere held a glint of green, and somewhere else almost too subtle for even the Princess's lonely wisdom, a glint of sorrow.

Then the Hind turned away, and the Princess touched her unspurred heels to her fleet young mare's sides, and followed silently. The Princess had a brief vision, though she did not stay to see, of the Hunt turning to make their sad and weary way homeward before they had even begun.

The Princess had no idea how long the chase lasted. The Hind wove swiftly through the close trees, and followed paths so narrow that the young mare's light feet could hardly find width enough to hold them; but while branches lashed at her and bushes held out twisted thorny hands to grab at her, the Princess found that she suffered little hurt; for some reason the forest let her pass, although the men who had ridden as she rode now had been less fortunate. The mare's neck and shoulders grew streaked with sweat and then with foam, but she still followed the Hind flashing through the green leaves before her with all the heart and spirit that was in her; for the love she bore her young mistress.

The sunlight began to cast different sorts of shadows

than it had in the morning; and the mare began to stumble, and her breathing was painful to hear. The Princess drew her up in pity, though her own spirit was mad for the following and she knew her horse would run till she fell dead if she were so asked. But the Hind paused too, and seemed to wait for them to catch her up; though her golden coat was unmarred, and her flanks moved easily with her light breathing.

All through that night they followed her; and there was moonlight enough to show those gilded flanks whenever they looked for their guide; the Princess had dismounted, and she and her horse faltered wearily on, and found each other's bleak and hungry company a comfort.

Just at dawn they staggered out from the edge of the forest—an edge they had not realized lay so near ahead, for the shadows of night had hidden it. But as the first blush of dawn aroused them, they stood blinking at the beginning of a land the Princess had never seen. There was grass before them, and scattered rocks, and a stream that ran babbling off into a distance they could not discern; and then looming up like a castle at the end of a field stood a mountain of bare grey rock. From where the Princess and her mare stood, they could see the green plain stretching out before them and to their right, up to the verge of the forest they had just crossed; but to the left, and standing against the last trees of the forest on that side, was this great hump of stone.

Before this mountain, only a few arm's-lengths away, stood the Hind. She waited till she caught the Princess's eye, and held her gaze for another moment while again they drank of each other's spirit; and then the Golden

Hind, who blazed up with a glory that could be hardly mortal as the morning sunlight found her, turned and disappeared into the rockface as if through a door.

The Princess dropped the bridle, and took a few steps after her; and then darkness came over her and she fell to the ground.

When she stirred again and turned her head to look around her, for a moment she had no idea where she was; the rough grass she lay on, the wild landscape around her were utterly unfamiliar; and then her mind began to clear and she sat up. The sun was near noon, and perhaps her faint had turned to sleep, for she felt a little rested, although still dizzy and uncertain; and she looked around first for her mare.

The mare had seen her sit up, and came toward her, holding her head delicately to one side so that she would not tread on the dragging reins, and her nostrils quivered in a little whicker of greeting. The Princess contrived to stand up by holding on to one of the long chestnut legs; and she stood for a moment with her head resting on the horse's shoulder. The sweat had dried, leaving the hair rough, but when the Princess raised her head and saw the mare with her own head turned to look back at her, she saw that the mare's eye was clear, and her bits were green and sticky with her grazing; and her breathing was untroubled.

"You're stronger than I am, my Lady," she said, "but then you have been standing in the stable and getting fat comfortably this last month . . ." and at that the Princess's mind cleared completely, and she remembered why she had come so far, and with what strange guide; and her head snapped around, and she stared at the grim grey pile before her, and she thought of the Hind, and her deep eyes and treacherous ways.

First she washed her face and hands in the running stream, and drank some of the sharp cold water, and when she stood up again she felt alert and well. Then she unsaddled and unbridled her horse and flung the harness indifferently on the ground; and paused to stroke the mare's forehead. "I'd be sorry to lose you, my Lady," she said, "but you know best; I can't say when . . . I can come back for you."

The mare nodded solemnly, and then stretched out a foreleg and lowered her head to rub her ears against it. The Princess turned to the steep stark mountain.

She remembered where the Hind had stood, and there she went, and examined the stone carefully; but she saw nothing that resembled a hidden door, and the hard grey surface appeared unbroken. She ran her hands over all till the fingertips were rough and sore; and still she found nothing. The mare had returned to her grazing, but occasionally she raised her head to watch the Princess curiously.

The sun set, and still the Princess knew not how next to seek her chosen adventure of the Hunting of the Hind; and as the shadows lengthened, rage rose in her, and despair; and she turned to see the half-moon floating up above the horizon. She looked at it for long enough that it rose several degrees of its arc; and then she closed her eyes and crossed her arms on her breast, turned, and walked straight into the rockface.

She had been standing less than an arm's-length away

from the side of the mountain as she stared at the moon; but now she walked forward—half a dozen steps, a dozen —but she feared to open her eyes to find herself caught by some magic a bodily part of the rock itself. So she continued forward, step by step, her eyes closed fast and her hands at her breast; and then she realized that her footsteps had begun to fall with an echo, as if she walked in a great cavern; and she opened her eyes.

It was a great cavern indeed; torches that gave off a fair and smokeless light were thrust in gold and ivory rings all around the walls, but the ceiling was lost in darkness at some immeasurable height. The walls, which from the clear light of the torches she could see to the height of cathedral walls, were of smooth stone, but that stone bore all the colors of the rainbow in its most peaceful and yet most joyful tints: yellows, greens, blues, and rosy reds; all were represented and all were glorious, and even the ever sharp thought of her dying brother was soothed a little as she looked.

The floor on which she walked was mirror smooth, and held a gleam of its own; but here was the shining of the sky before a storm, thunderheads of majestic white and heavy grey; and her booted feet struck out a noise like the ringing of a bell with every step.

Then she saw, still far away from her, a low wall, she thought perhaps in the center of this great place, for it was far away from the walls she could see. And on the wall, with its head bowed, sat a figure draped in white.

As the Princess approached, she realized that the shining golden head of the figure was no crown nor work of man's hands, but the fabulous masses of heavy golden hair.

When she grew near, the figure looked up: and her eyes met deep brown eyes with a glint of green in their depths, and a glint that the Princess saw more clearly now, of sorrow. And as the Princess saw the pale perfect face that held those eyes, she remembered her brother's words, "I have seen her"; and her legs folded under her, and she knelt at the feet of a woman whose beauty could send a man mad, or blind, but grateful in his blindness, or even comfortable in his madness.

"Please, you must not kneel; it is not fit," said the woman. "Indeed, I know I am very beautiful, for I cannot help knowing; nor can I help the beauty, which is not even rightfully mine."

The Princess rose slowly, and looked bewildered at the woman who had made such a curious speech; and, at her gesture, sat on the wall near her. "Do not fear me," the woman went on gently, as she read the puzzlement in the face before her; "you have looked into my eyes, and seen that I am—I am like you, whatever my face may say; and I thank you—I thank you exceedingly for that favor." She paused. "He who keeps me here . . . lent my own, my human beauty, a touch of horror and dread, that I should fill the hearts of those who look on me with a wildness of delight that would destroy them."

"Why?" said the Princess; and her whisper seemed to run out to the sheer walls, and even through them, carrying her question she could not guess where.

"Because I refused him," said the woman, but her reply went only into the Princess's ears, and to nothing that might wait beyond the walls. "And so he decided that none should have me; and that the face that had caught him would grow hateful to its owner for what it did to others . . ." and the woman covered her glorious, terrible face with her hands, and tears like diamonds slid through her fingers.

"What may I do for you?" said the Princess. "I am here to help you, for my brother's sake." But her voice trembled; for while no dread had touched her heart, because she had seen past this woman's beauty into the deeps of her spirit in the green flickers of her wide eyes, still there was a fearfulness to the magnificence of the cavern, and she felt the weight of the woman's cursed beauty as a soldier might feel a weight on his sword arm.

"Tell me what to do, and I will try, as best I may." And the Princess realized as she spoke that while it was love for her brother that had brought her to dare as she did, still she was moved with sympathy for this strange woman, and would wish to help her if she could.

"For your brother's sake," said the woman, and a half-smile touched her sadness. "I have a brother too. Come." She stood up, and the Princess stood too; but reeled in her place, and the woman reached out an exquisite white hand and caught her. "Come. You shall meet my brother, and you shall have something to eat, for I see you are faint with hunger, and I know too well the cause of it. Then perhaps we can tell you how you may save us all—" and the Princess heard the desperate anxiety in that sweet voice, and realized how sharply the woman had to catch herself up when she spoke of that hope.

They walked, the Princess leaning on the woman's arm, toward one of the gorgeous colored walls; and as they approached, there was a plain simple doorway in the rock that the Princess could see and touch and understand, and she sighed as they passed through it.

They found themselves in a small room, and a golden smokeless fire like the fire of the torches glowed in a hollow at one end of it, and a man sat at a table at the center of it; and on that table were bread and cheese and fruit, and pitchers and cups and plates. The man stood up to welcome them, and the Princess saw that he was lame; he came no more than two steps toward them, and that only by leaning heavily on the table.

"Welcome, Princess," he said, and his eyes were brown and green like his sister's, and held the same imprisoned sorrow. He stretched out his hands and took the Princess's between them for a moment, and for that little moment she thought a little less about her brother, as she had when she first looked at the rainbow walls of the cavern. "First you must eat," said this man.

And so the Princess sat down, and ate white bread and yellow cheese, and fruits of green and red and deep blue-purple, and the woman of the terrible beauty ate with her, as did that woman's brother, although the Princess noticed that they ate very little.

When they had finished, and the Princess stared into her cup without drinking, the man said gently: "My name is Darin, and my sister is Sellena. This place is a place of much magic, and little of that good, but you may trust us with your name without fear. Will you give it us?"

The Princess looked up and answered at once: "My name is Korah."

There was silence a moment, and Sellena reached

across the table to touch the Princess's hand. "Thank you. We have not heard another name beyond our own in this place for many a long year."

"You are welcome to it," said the Princess, and smiled; and she thought, as something that was almost an answering smile hovered like a shadow over Sellena's mouth, that it was the first time in many a long year that a smile had been seen in this place either.

"Now that I have eaten," said the Princess, "and we hold each other's names, will you not tell me something of your durance here?" and her hands tightened involuntarily around the cup she held.

"I am sent out as the Hind again and again whether I will or nay," Sellena burst out; and in her voice was anger and helplessness and pleading mixed, "for he who holds us here loves to prove his power again and again with each new victim I bring him. And yet there is no other hope of our ever winning free but to go out as he wills, in the guise of a brute beast, and lure those who will come. And every failure weighs on my heart, for it is I who lead each to his destruction, however little I wish it to fall out so."

"I tried once to free her," said Darin in a low voice. "Even I: indeed, I was the first. I do not know if perhaps the wizard had not yet fully formed his plans, for I escaped with my mind, and only he lamed my leg; so I may think, but may not walk. And I am permitted to keep my sister company in her exile, and no further harm has he tried to do me. But perhaps it amuses him best so, to see the two or us clinging to each other in our powerlessness to resist him; and I do not know if it is a blessing to be spared, spared to watch all the brave hunters going to their doom."

"It is a blessing to me, brother," said Sellena softly; and Darin bowed his head.

Then the Princess said to them both as she had said to Sellena alone: "What may I do for you? For I will take my turn, and seek to free you, if I may."

Darin answered soberly, "You must go to him who keeps us here and ask him to let us go."

The Princess looked at him, and his eyes were grave. "It sounds an easy task, does it not? And yet there have been hundreds who followed the Golden Hind to this mountain. Some few of those, and of them we have no counting, have lost all but their lives in just the sight of the Golden Hind, and they go home tired and dreaming, and so spend the years remaining to them without strength or will. Some of those who track the Hind to the walls of this mountain do find their way inside. Some few of these cannot bear the sight of Sellena as you see her, for the dread wizard did lay upon her beauty; and even those who bear it are dazzled by it, so they cannot hold their spirits still within them when they go to face the enchanter. Of those six-and-thirty who have passed through the wizard's chamber, eleven have died, and so completely did the wizard destroy them that not even their bodies remained to be given burial; and the other five-and-twenty returned to their lives and homes mad."

"All but the last," Sellena said, in a voice so low that it was scarcely audible; and the Princess stiffened in her chair.

"All but the last," repeated Darin; "but I fear that the

wound he received will still prove mortal."

Sellena covered her beautiful face with her hands and moaned.

"That last was my brother," said the Princess; "he lies on his bed dying even now, if he is not yet dead. He is why I am here."

Again Sellena reached across the table to touch the Princess's hand; but this time Sellena spoke no word, and though the hand trembled, it did not move away.

"He whom you must ask for our freedom," said Darin, "will turn whatever is in you against you. The greater your strength, the graver the wound you will receive from the weapon he will forge of it. You must go to him empty, drained of all that is your spirit and your heart and your mind; you must be an empty shell carrying only the question: 'Will you set the two you hold in bondage free?'"

The Princess stared at Darin. "Tell me one thing first, and then I will go as you bid me. What happened to my brother?"

It was Sellena who answered: "He looked into my eyes, even as you did—and as none other ever has; by this I should have recognized your kinship. But as you saw only that my spirit was like unto yours and could see in me a sister, he—he loved me. I, who have never been loved so, for my perilous beauty has blinded all those that look at it: all but Darin my brother, and you, Korah my sister—and that one other. Your brother, who lies dying for it." And another diamond tear crept down her glowing cheek.

"He escaped sick and strengthless only," said Darin, "because for all the strength of the love he suddenly found for my sister, it was of a clarity even the wizard could not bend entirely against him; and so he lost neither his life nor his sanity by it." Then Darin turned frowning to the Princess and said: "This must have been a great blow to the vanity of this enchanter, who has shattered all who have approached him during our long keeping; and I fear for the sister of him who dealt that blow, for the added malice the wizard will hold toward anyone of the same blood."

The Princess shook her head, just a tremor, right to left, for she feared to shake tears over the brink of her eyelids. "Still I will go, and fear no more than I must. The sickness laid upon my brother is a wasting fever that no doctor can halt; and he will yet . . . die, of that wizard's work." She turned her eyes, still bright with tears, to meet Darin's quiet eyes, seeking comfort, and comfort she found. She let herself sink into their green depths and felt that she could rest there forever; and even as she felt Darin's spirit reaching to touch hers, she remembered Sellena's words: *He—he loved me;* and she shook herself free with a gasp.

Darin at once covered his eyes with a hand, and bowed his head. "Forgive me," he said, and his voice was deep with an emotion the Princess chose not to hear; "I—I had no thought of this."

"Where is the wizard's cell?" said the Princess; and her breast rose and fell with her quick breathing. "Will you show me where I must enter? I do not wish to tarry."

She looked at Sellena, and did not permit even the flick of a glance to where Darin sat with his dark eyes still behind his hand.

"Yes. Come." The two women stood up; Darin remained motionless as Sellena opened another door in the small chamber in which they had sat, not the one they had entered by. Across this threshold it was very dark. Sellena took the Princess's hand to lead her. "I know the way and will not stumble. It is better without light, for the walls here are similar to those in the cavern where you met me, but the colors will lead you to confusion if you look at them long." And down the dark road they went, hand in hand; their breathing and their soft footsteps were the only sounds.

"Here," said Sellena at last. "I can take you no farther." The blackness was perfect; the Princess could see not the vaguest outline of the woman who stood beside her, but she could tell by the sound of her voice that Sellena had turned to face her. "There is no danger here, in this simple dark; but your next step will begin your final journey which will take you to the wizard's den, and once you have taken that step you will be able neither to stop nor to turn back.

"Stand here awhile, till everything you are, everything you think and remember and feel, drains out of you. What my brother told you of the wizard's ways is true. Even when you think you have left yourself like a discarded cloak, wait—search again, into every corner of your being; you must not leave even a shred of your personality for the wizard to seize upon. He will search you like the dagger in the hand of the assassin. What you leave here, I will hold for you in the palms of my hands, and I will wait here for your return and give these things up to you again just as they were when you left them in my keeping. Your heart and your hopes are safe here with me, but you must not take them with you, for he whom you will face will make spears of them and drive them back upon you."

The Princess stood awhile, with the blackness standing all around her; and she remembered all of the months that had gone to make up her tally of seventeen years; and each week of those months she remembered. She remembered how she had learned to leave her heart behind her when she was summoned by her father, because his lack of love for her hurt her; and how she had only taken up her heart again gladly, and joined it to her hopes and fears, when she went to meet her brother. And she thought of her brother and how he had never understood the hurtfulness of love, so that when he discovered a great love in the eyes of Sellena he had not been able to lay it aside when he went to face the wizard; and now he lay dying of his weakness, of his simple honesty.

She thought of all these things, and then she felt Sellena's hands on her face; and silently she yielded up all of her that was hers to Sellena's care, saving only the question she must ask the wizard. And she felt her body as dark and empty as the tunnel she stood in, with herself and Sellena the questions who waited their asking, and she took the first step of the last stage of her journey to the wizard.

She was dimly aware of a roaring in her ears, and heat

against her skin that came and went, and a flickering like lightning in her eyes; but she had left herself no thoughts to think, and she did not think of these things. She could not even count the steps she took, but she came at last to a lighted place, a cavern, low and white, and at the center of the cavern was a chair of white rock that seemed to grow up out of the floor without break or joint. The white light, for which there was no source visible, burnt fiercely upon the face of the figure that sat in the chair; and the face and the figure bore the semblance of a man. He wore long black robes that covered all but his long white fingers and pale face; a hood was pulled over his head and low upon his brow, but his eyes glared at her, bright with rage and brighter with power. But she had no names for these things now, and so she did not try to name them; nor had she left herself fear, and so the frenzy in the face before her inspired in her no fear.

She opened her mouth, and gave utterance to the one thing she had brought with her to the wizard's lair: "Will you set the two you hold in bondage free?"

The chair, and the creature on it, and the cavern itself disappeared; silently and seemingly gently, for the Princess felt no shock; it was as though she watched a shape of snow melt in spring sunshine. She blinked, and found herself . . . somewhere else; and the first thing she knew was Sellena's hands again on her face, and all that Sellena had held safe for her ran back inside her and made her breathe quickly for joy; for the first thing she then did was turn to Darin, who stood at Sellena's side, lame no longer, but standing strong on both feet.

And Darin and Korah looked long and deep in one another's eyes.

Then they turned away to see Sellena's eyes shining brightly on both of them together; and they all three laughed, and Darin and the Princess blushed, and then they looked around to see where they were. But Darin's and the Princess's hands somehow met and clasped, while their eyes were busy elsewhere.

The grey grim mountain was gone, and they stood on a sweet green plain untroubled by rough stone and starry with flowers, and a stream ran off to their right, and before them was the forest. And the Princess's chestnut mare came running to greet them.

"We must return to your city," said Sellena, and her eyes were shining still, but the thoughts behind them were changed. It was only then that the Princess saw the warm beauty of her friend and sister, and knew that she had been healed too. "For as my brother's leg is whole again, so—so many other things come right."

The Princess drew her mare's head down to her own breast a moment, and whispered in the chestnut ears that flicked forward to listen. "Go," she said then to Sellena. "Ride my mare; she will take you as swiftly as she may to my home and hers; and we will follow after." And the Princess bridled and saddled her horse, and Sellena mounted and rode off.

The forest did not seem wide to the two who followed behind; and though they walked swiftly, it was gaily too, and without thought of weariness nor any desire that the journey come to an end. But the dense undergrowth that had stretched on and on almost without measure when the Princess had followed the Hind gave way now to tall easy-spaced trees and frequent meadows full of singing birds; and the two that walked on had not by any means come to the end of all they had to say to each other when they found they had come to the end of the trees. They emerged from the forest just in time to see the party that was setting out from the city to meet them. In that party rode the thirteenth hunter, who reined his horse so close to his wife's that he might hold her hand as if he would never let it free again; and at their head rode the Prince, who was perhaps thinner than he should be, but he rode his tall stallion with his old grace and strength, and at his side rode Sellena. And behind the two that stepped out of the forest stepped several more, eleven in all, whose presence had not been suspected even by themselves, for they had thought themselves long dead in a wizard's cave. But now they strode forward to bow to the Prince and ask the way to their homes and countries, barring the two who belonged to this kingdom, and who wept for joy at finding themselves in it again; and they all did homage to her who had rescued them.

The
Twelve
Dancing
Princesses

PROLOGUE

ONCE THERE WAS a soldier, who was a good man and a brave one; but somehow he did not prosper in a soldier's life. For he was a poor man, the son of a poor farmer; and when he wished to join the Army, at the age of eighteen, bright with hope and youth and strength, the only regiment that would have him, a poor man's son, was a regiment that could not keep its ranks filled. This regiment was commanded by a colonel who was a hard man; he bullied his men because he was himself afraid, and so his regiment was shunned by the best men, for none wished to serve under this colonel, but because he was a very wealthy man, none could seek to replace him.

But the young farmer's son knew nothing of this; and so he signed his name to the regiment's papers, freely and joyfully, waiting only to be asked to do his best.

But twenty years passed, and the farmer's son became an old soldier; he lost his youth and much of his health and strength, and gained nothing worth having in their place. For his colonel had soon learned of the fineness of the new man under his command; and the colonel's pride and weakness could not bear the sight of such strength in a farmer's son. And the colonel sent him on the most dangerous missions, and made sure that he was always standing in the first rank of his company when it was thrown into battle; and the farmer's son always did his best, but the best that he was given in return was his bare life.

And so at the end of twenty years the soldier left his regiment and left the Army, for he was stiff with many wounds; and, worse, he was weary and sad at heart, with a sadness that had no hope in it anywhere.

He shouldered the small bundle that held in it all that he owned in the world; and he walked down the first road he came to. And so he wandered aimlessly from one week to the next; for his father had died long ago, and his brother tilled the farm, and the soldier did not want to disturb his family's quiet happiness with his grey weariness.

As he wandered through the hills, he found himself going slowly but steadily downhill, like a small rivulet that searches for its own level, seeks a larger stream that will in turn spill it into the river; but where the river flowed at last into the sea stood the tall pale city of the King. And the soldier, as he bought himself meals and a hayloft to sleep in by doing small jobs for the people he met—and he found, however slow the last twenty years had made him, that his hands and back still knew how to lift and heave a pitchfork, how to back a skittish horse to a plough or a wagon—he found in him also a strange and rootless desire to leave the mountains for the first time in his life, to descend to the lowlands and go at last to the King's city at the mouth of the river, and see the castle of the man for whom he had worked, nameless, all the years of his youth. He would look upon the King's house, and perhaps even see his face for a moment as he rode in his golden carriage among his people. For the soldier's regiment had been a border regiment, patrolling the high wild mountains beyond the little hill farms like the one he had grown up on; and the only faces of his countrymen that he had seen were those of other soldiers; the only towns, barracks and mess halls and stables.

As he went slowly downhill he began to hear bits of a story that told of an enchantment that had been laid on the twelve beautiful daughters of the King.

At first the tale was only told in snatches, for it was of little interest to farmers, who have enough to think about with the odd ways of the weather, of crops, of animals—and possibly of wives and sons and their own daughters. But in the first town he came to, big enough to have a main street with an inn on it, instead of the highland villages which were no more than half a dozen thatched cottages crouched together on the cheek of some gentler hill: at this town he stopped for a time and worked as an ostler, and here he heard the story of the Princesses in full from another ostler.

The King had twelve daughters and no sons; and perhaps this was a sorrow to him, but perhaps not; for sons may fight over their father's crown—even before he is decently dead. And these twelve Princesses were each more beautiful than the last, no matter how one counted them. The Queen had died giving birth to a thirteenth daughter, who died with her; that was ten years ago, now. And it was only a little after the Queen's death that the trouble began.

The youngest Princess was then only eight years of age, and the Princesses' dancing-master had only begun to instruct her; although truth to tell, these girls seemed to have been born with the knowledge of the patterns of the dance written in them somewhere. A royal household must have a dancing-master; but the master who taught these twelve Princesses had the lightest labor of anyone in the castle, although he was a superb artist himself and could have taught them a great deal if they had needed it. But they did not; and so he smiled, and nodded, and waved his music-wand occasionally, and thought of other things.

Sometime during the youngest Princess's ninth year it was observed that during the night, every night, the dancing shoes of the twelve Princesses were worn through, with holes in the heels, and across the tender balls of the feet. And every morning all the cobblers of the city had to set aside their other work and make up twelve new pairs of dancing shoes by the evening; for it was not to be thought of that the Princesses should do without, even for a day. And every morning those twelve new pairs of delicate dancing slippers were worn quite through.

After this had gone on for some weeks the King called all his daughters to him at once and looked at them sternly, for all that he loved them dearly, or perhaps because of it: and he demanded to know where it was they danced their nights away till they wore their grace-

ful shoes to tatters that could only be tossed away. And
all but the eldest Princess hung their heads and the
youngest wept; the eldest looked back at her father as
he looked at her, but hers was a glance he could not
read. And none of them spoke a word.

Then the King grew angry in his love for them which
made him afraid: and he shouted at them, but still they
gave him no answer.

And then he sent them away, dismissed them as he
would servants, with a flick of his hand, and no gentle
words as he was used to give them; and they went. If
they dragged their feet at all, in sorrow or in shame, the
soles of their shoes were so soft they made no sound.
Their father, the King, sat silent on his throne for a long
space after they had left, his head bowed in his hand, and
his eyes shaded from the sight of his courtiers. The
courtiers wondered what he might be thinking; and they
remembered the Queen, for she was then but recently
gone, and wondered if there was anything she might
have done.

At last the King stirred, and he gave orders: that the
Princesses henceforward should all sleep in the same
room; and that room would be the Long Gallery. And
the Long Gallery should be fitted at once with the
Princesses' twelve beds and thirty-six wardrobes. And
that the windows should be barred in iron, and the door
also; and the door fitted with a great iron lock to which
only one key would be made; and that key would be
hung around the King's neck on a long black leather
thong.

This was done; and although the carpenters and ironmongers were well paid, they had no joy in their work; and the blacksmith who had made the single heavy lock for the door and the key for the King's own neck would take no payment for them whatsoever, and he went back to his own shop on the far side of the city with a slow tread, and spoke to no one for three days after. There were rumors, whispered uneasily, that the castle had shaken underfoot with more than the blows of the craftsmen's hammers while the work went forward; but no one quite dared to mention this openly, and no one was quite happy with the idea that they were imagining things.

And still the Princesses' shoes were worn through every morning. And it was seen that the Princesses grew pale and still paler within their imprisonment, and spoke rarely—even the youngest, who had been used to roll hoops down the long, echoing Long Gallery when it was still an open way, and chase them laughing. The Princesses laughed no longer; but they grew no less beautiful. The eldest in particular held the dignity of a lioness caged in her wide deep eyes and in her light step. And the King looked after his daughters with longing, and often he saw them looking back at him; but they would not speak.

Then the King sought out all the wise men of his land and asked them if they could discover anything about the enchantment—if enchantment it be, and how could it not?—that his daughters went under, and how it might be broken. And the wise men looked into their magic mirrors and their odd-colored smokes, and drank strange ill-smelling brews and looked at the backs of their own eyelids; and called up their familiars, and even wrestled with dark spells that were nearly too much for their strength, and spoke to creatures better left alone, who hissed and babbled and shrieked. And they spoke to their King again, shaking their heads. Little enough they had to tell him: that spell it was there was no doubt; and that it was one too strong for them to destroy in the usual ways, with powders and weird words, was also, sadly, beyond doubt; and several of them shivered and rubbed their hands together as they said this.

The King looked at them for a long moment in silence, and then asked in a voice so low that if they had not been wise men they might not have heard it at all: "Is there, then, no hope?"

One who had not spoken before stepped forward; his hair was grey, and his long robe a smoke-draggled green. He looked at the King for a time, almost as if he had forgotten the language he must use, and then he said: "I can offer you this much. If someone, someone not of the Princesses' blood kin, can discover where they dance all night, and bring the tale back to this earth, tell it under this sun—for you may be sure that this dark place knows neither—with some token of that land, then the enchantment shall be broken. For I deem that its strength depends upon its remaining hidden."

The King whispered: "Not of their blood kin?"

The wise man looked upon him with what, had he been anyone but the King, might have been pity. "Sire," he said gently, "one of the Princesses' blood would only fall under the same sorcery that enthralls them. They are still your daughters, even as they move through the web that has been woven around them. What that sorcery might do to another—we cannot tell. But if he lived, he would not be free."

The King nodded his head slowly and turned away to begin the journey back to his haunted castle. And when he returned he gave more orders: that any man who discovered where the Princesses danced their shoes to pieces each night should have his choice of them for a wife, and reign as king after his wife's father died. Any man who wished to try was welcome: king's son or cobbler, curate or knight or ploughman. And each of them, whatever his rank, should have an equal chance; and that chance was to spend three nights on a cot set up in the Princesses' locked chamber; three nights, no more nor any less.

A king's son came first; he was the son of a king from just over the border that the soldier's regiment had fought for; but, for all that, he was graciously welcomed, and fed the same dishes that were set before the King and his daughters; and there was music to entertain them all as they sat silently at their meal, and later there were jugglers and acrobats, but no dancers; and the music was stately or brisk, but it was never dancing music, and the King and the Princesses and their guest sat quietly at the high table.

When the time came to retire, the King clasped a rich red robe around the shoulders of the son of his old enemy with his own hands, and wished him well, kindly and honestly; and showed him where he would spend his three nights. A bed had been set up at the end of the Long Gallery, behind a screen; and besides a bed and a blanket and the robe around his shoulders he was given a lamp, for it was dark at the end of the Gallery. And the King embraced him and left him; and there was perfect silence in the long room as thirteen pairs of ears listened to the heavy door swing shut and the King's key turn in the lock.

But somehow the king's son fell asleep that night; and in the morning the Princesses' shoes were worn through. And so went the second night; and even the third. On that last night the king's son wished so much to stay awake and see how the Princesses did that he never lay down at all. But in the morning he was discovered to have fallen asleep nonetheless, still on his feet, leaning heavily against the rough stone wall, so that his cheek was marked by the stone, and so harshly that the bruise did not fade for days after.

The prince went away, pale behind the red stain on his face, and he was not seen again.

Here the ostler paused in his story, and stared at the soldier, who was listening with an attention he had not felt since his first years in the Army. "You'll hear that our King cuts off the heads of them who fail to guess the Princesses' riddle. But it's not so. They fade away sometimes so quickly it's as if they have been murdered; but it's not our King puts his hand to it, nor do I believe another story that has it that the Princesses poison them to keep their secret. All that is nonsense. The way of it is just that they have to meet our King's eyes when they tell him that they've failed; and the look he gives them back has all a father's sorrow in it, and all a king's pride —and all our King's goodness, and it takes the heart right out of them that have to see it. And so they leave, but there's no heart left in them for anything." The ostler

shrugged; and the soldier smiled, and then stood up and
sighed and stretched, for the story had been a long one
—and then thoughtfully collected his and his friend's
tankards and disappeared for a moment into the taproom.
When he returned with two brimming mugs, the ostler
was examining a headstall with disfavor: the new stable
boy had cleaned it, and done a poor job. He would be
spoken to tomorrow, and if that didn't work, on the next
day, kicked. But he dropped the reins happily to take up
his beer; and as he looked at his new friend over the
brim there was a new flicker behind his eyes.

"And what are you thinking?" he said at last.

"You already know or you would not ask," replied the
soldier. "I'm thinking that I would like to see the city of
our King, the King in whose Army I labored so long and
for so little. And I'm thinking that I would like to find
out the secret of the shoes that are danced to pieces
every night, and so win a Princess to wife and a kingdom
after." He smiled at the ostler, hoping to win an answering smile. "It is perhaps my only chance to try to see
the ways of the Army hierarchy set to rights."

The ostler slowly shook his head without smiling, but
he said no word to dissuade him. "Good luck to you then
my wild and wandering friend. But if your luck should
not be good, then come back here, and we'll try to save
you with good horses and good beer. They can if anything can."

"I have little enough heart left in me now," said the
soldier lightly. "The King is welcome to the rest, for I'll
not miss it."

And on the next morning the soldier set out.

PART ONE

HE WENT still downhill, but more purposefully; and the bundle across his shoulders was a little stouter, thanks to the ostler. He cut himself a green walking-stick by the bank of the brook his path led him beside; and the sap ran over his hand, and the sweet sharp smell of it raised his spirits. He whistled as he walked, Army songs, songs about death and glory.

The sun was high in the sky and the place of his waking miles behind him when the soldier began to look around him for somewhere to sit and eat his lunch; he hoped for a stream of clear mountain water; if luck was with him he would find a wide-branching tree at its edge to sit beneath, for the sun grew hot, and shade would be welcome. The soldier's boots began to scuff up the dust of the lowlands as the hard rocky earth of the mountains was left behind him. He had passed through several villages on his long morning's walk, for the villages sat close together at the mountains' green feet. But as he looked around now for his stream and his tree, he saw grazing land, with cows and sheep and horses on it, and

fields of grain; and far off to his left he could see the hard
shining of the river that led to the capital that was also
his path's end. But there were few houses. He looked
ahead, and saw a small grove of trees, and quickened his
step, anticipating at least their leafy shadow, and perhaps
a pool of water.

As he approached he heard an odd creaking noise that
began, and stopped, and began again; but the trees hid
from his sight anything that his eyes might discover to explain it. When his way led by them at last, he saw a small
hut nestled within the grove, and before it and near his
path stood a well. An old woman stood at the well, winding up the rope with a handle that creaked; and she
paused often and wearily, and as the soldier watched
she, unknowing, stared into the depths of the well and
sighed.

"May I help you?" said the soldier, and strode forward
and he seized the handle from the brown wrinkled hand
that gladly gave it up to him, and wound the handle till
the bucket tipped past the stone lip of the well; and he
pulled it out, brimming, and set it on the ground.

"I thank you, good sir," said the old woman. "And
beg you then, have the first draught; for I should be
waiting a long time yet for my drink if I had to wait
upon my own drawing of it. I believe the bucket grows
heavier each day, even faster than the strength drains
away from my old hand."

The soldier pulled the knapsack from his shoulder, and
from it took a battered tin cup: one of the scant relics of
his Army days. He picked up the old woman's brown
pottery cup from the edge of the well and dipped them

both together; and as he handed her dripping cup to her he held his own; and they drank together.

The woman smiled. "Such courtesy demands better recompense than a poor old woman can offer," she said. "Rest yourself in the shade of these trees a little while, at least, and tell me where so gallant a gentleman may be bound." She looked straight at him as she spoke, and when he smiled at her words she must have noticed the strength and sweetness in his smile, for all the weariness of the face that held it; and certain it is that, as he smiled, he noticed the strange eyes of the woman who stared at him so straightforwardly. Her eyes were a blue that was almost lavender, and they held a calm that seemed to bear more of the innocence of youth than the gravity of age. And the lashes were long, as long as a fawn's, and dark.

"Indeed, I will be most grateful for a chance to sit out of the sun's light." And they sat together on a rough wooden bench under a tree near the tiny cottage; and the soldier told the old woman of his journey, and, thinking of her strange eyes—for he spoke with his eyes on the ground between his knees—he also told her of its purpose, for the thought came to him that behind those eyes there might be some wisdom to help him on his way. In the pause that followed his telling, he offered her some of his bread and cheese, and they ate silently.

At last, and trying not to be disappointed by her silence, the soldier said that he would go on; for he could walk many more miles that day before he would need another meal, and sleep to follow. This much his soldier's training had done for him. And he stood up, and picked up his knapsack to tie it to its place on his back again.

"Wait a moment," said the old woman; and he waited, gladly. She walked—swiftly, for a woman so old and weak that she had trouble drawing up her bucket from the well—the few steps to her cottage, and disappeared within. She was gone long enough that the soldier began to feel foolish for his sudden hope that she was a wise woman after all and would assist him. "Probably she is gone to find for me some keepsake trinket, a clay dog, a luck charm made of birds' feathers, that she has not seen in years and has forgotten where it lies," he said to himself. "But perhaps she will give me bread and cheese for what she has eaten of mine; and that will be welcome; for cities, I believe, are not often friendly to a poor wanderer."

But it was none of these things she held in her hands when she returned to him. It was, instead, a cape; she carried it spilled over her arms, and shook it out for him when she stood beside him again by the bench and the tree. The cape was long enough to sweep the ground even when she held it arm's-length over her head; and a deep hood fell from its collar. It was black with a blackness that denied sunlight; it looked like a hole in the earth's own substance, as if, had one the alien eyes for it, one could see into the far reaches of some other awful world within it. And it moved to its own shaken air, as if it breathed like an animal.

The soldier looked at it with awe, for it was an uncanny thing. The old woman said: "Take this as my gift to you, and consider your time spent telling me your story time spent well, for I can thus give you a gift to serve your purpose. This cloak is woven of the shadows that hide the hare from the fox, the mouse from the hawk, and the lovers from those who would forbid their love. Wear it and you are invisible: for the cloak is close-woven, finer than loose shadows, and no rents will betray you. See—" and the old woman whirled it around her own bowed shoulders, shaking the hood down over her bright eyes—and then the soldier saw nothing where she stood, or had stood, but the dappled, moving leaf-shade over the grass and wildflowers and the rough wooden bench. He blinked and felt suddenly cold, and then as suddenly hot: hot with the hope that blazed up in him and need not, this time, be quelled.

A whirling of air become shadow, become untouched entire blackness, and the old woman stood before him again, holding the cloak in her hands, and it poured over her feet. "—or not see," she said, and smiled. "Take it." She held it out to him. It was as weightless as the shadows it was made of, soft as night; he wound it gently round his hands, and it turned itself to a wisp like a lady's scarf; and gently he tucked it under a shoulder strap of his knapsack. It whispered to itself there, and one silken corner waved against his cheek.

"I have words to send with you too," said the old woman. "First: speak not of me, nor of this cloak," and she looked at him shrewdly. "But you may guess that for yourself. You may guess this too: drink nothing the Princesses may offer you when you retire to your cot in the dark corner of the Long Gallery. It is a wonder and an amazement to me that the men before you have not thought of this simple trick; but it is said otherwise—and I, I have my ways of hearing the truth."

"Perhaps it is the youth of those men," said the soldier gravely; "for I have heard that all those who have sought this riddle and the prize have been young and fair to look upon. I have little of either youth or beauty to spend, and must make it up in caution."

The old woman laughed oddly, and looked at him still more oddly, the leaf-shadow moving in her eyes like silver fish in a lake. "Perhaps it is as you say. Or perhaps it is something that stands with the Princess as she offers the drink; something that is loosened in that Long Gallery once the key in the door has turned and this world, our world, is locked away for the night's length." There was something in her face like pain or sorrow.

"For this too I wish to say to you: the Princesses you must beware, for the spell they lie under is deep, and spell it truly is, but neither of their making nor their fault, and very glad they would be to be free of it, though they may stir no hand to help themselves." The old woman paused so long that the soldier thought she might not speak again, and he listened instead to the shadowy whispering at his ear, and let his eyes wander to the path that would take him to the city, and to his chosen adventure and his fate.

"The story is this, as I believe it," said the old woman; "and as I have told you, I have ways of hearing the truth.

"The Queen had the blood of witches in her," she went on slowly, "and while the taint is ancient and feeble, still it was there; while the King is mortal clear through, or if there is any other dilution, it is so old that even the witches themselves have forgotten, and so can do nothing.

"The Queen was a good woman, and she was mortal and human, and bore mortal daughters. The drop of witch blood was like a chink in the armor of a knight rather than a poison at the heart. The knight may be valiant in arms and honor as was the Queen in honor and love; but the spear of an enemy will find the chink at last.

"There is a sort of charm in witch blood for those who bear it; a charm to make the spears that may fly go awry. But the charm weakens faster than the blood taint itself if the bearer chooses mortal ways and never leaves them.

"In the Queen there was something yet left in that charm. In her daughters—nay. And so when the Queen died, a witch seized her chance: that her twelve demon sons, who bear a taint of mortal blood as faint as the witch blood of the Queen's twelve daughters, those sons shall be tied to those daughters closely and more closely, till by their grasp they shall be drawn from the deeps where they properly live to the sweet earth's surface; and there they shall marry the twelve Princesses, and beget upon them children in whom the dark blood shall run hot and strong for many generations, and who shall wreak much woe upon simple men.

"Eleven years will it take for the witch's dark chain to be forged from Princes to Princesses, till the Princesses return one morning with the witch's sons at their sides; eleven years' dancing underground. And nine and a half years already have run of this course."

The soldier grew pale beneath his sun-brown skin as

he heard the old woman's words. "Do any but you know of this? You—and now I?"

The old woman shrugged, but it was half a shiver, the soldier thought, and wondered; for a wise woman usually fears not what she knows. "The Princesses know, but they cannot tell. The King knows not, for the knowledge would break him to no purpose, for the quest and the venture are not his. For the rest, I myself know not; those fools the King consulted when the trouble first began may know a little; but they knew at least not to tell the King anything he could not bear. And you are the only one I have told." The old woman again lifted her long-lashed eyes to the soldier, and the silver fish in her lakewater eyes had turned gold with the intensity of her telling.

"And the Princesses can do nothing," repeated the soldier, "nothing but watch the sands of their own time running out." The soldier thought of battles, and how it was the waiting that made men mad, and that to risk life and limb crossing bloody swords on the battlefield was joyful beside it.

"The eldest, it is said," the old woman said even more slowly, "has more of wit than her sisters; and yet even she cannot put out a hand to save herself one night's journey underground, nor even fail to give the man who would free her the drugged wine when he retires to his cot in the dark corner of the Gallery." The old woman turned her eyes to the path the soldier would follow, that would lead him to the city, and the King's pale castle, and the twelve dancing Princesses.

He was miles down that road, the corner of the cloak

of shadows caressing his cheek, before he thought to wonder if he had bade the old woman farewell. He could not remember.

He spent that night in the open, under the stars, at the edge of a small wood; and he ate his bread and cheese, and stared into the impenetrable forest shadows that were yet less black than his cloak. But when he lay down, he fell asleep instantly, with the instincts of an old soldier; and the same instinct gave him as much rest as he might have from his sleep, and swept his dreams free of demons and princesses and old women at wells. He dreamed instead of his friend the ostler, and of sharp brown beer.

He arrived at the capital city in the late afternoon of the following day. The streets were full of people, some shouting, some driving animals; some silent, some alone, some talking to those who walked beside them. The soldier had noticed, when he rose on the morning of this his last day's journey, that the ways he walked held more people than those he had trod recently; and there is a bustle and a stirring to city-bound folk that is like no other restlessness. By this if nothing else the country-wise farmer's son and old campaigner would have known his way.

He was one of the silent and solitary ones as he passed the city gates: at which stood guards, stiff and wordless as axles, staring across the gap they framed like statues of conquerors. He looked around him, and listened. The streets were wide and well paved, and he saw few beggars, and those quiet ones, who stayed at their chosen street

corners with their begging-bowls extended and their eyes
calmly lowered. The buildings were all several stories
high; but there were many trees, too, green-leafed and
full, and frequent parks, each with its titular statue of an
historical hero. The soldier made his way slowly from
the eastern gate, where he had entered, to the river, which
lay a little west of the center of the city. At the river's bank
he paused, then stepped off the path and went down to
the very edge of the whispering water.

Here he saw the King's castle for the first time. It stood
near the mouth of the river, on the far bank, so the river
gleamed like silver before it, and behind it one caught the
green-and-grey glitter of the sea, stretching out beyond
the castle's broad grounds. The vastness of that glitter,
reaching the horizon without a ripple, accepting the
river's great waters without a murmur, made the castle
seem a toy, and all the lands and their borders for which
men fought, a minor and unimportant interruption of the
tides. The soldier, staring, for a moment forgot his quest;
forgot even his beloved mountains, and his twenty wasted
years. He shook himself free, set himself to study the
castle of the King, and of the twelve dancing Princesses.

It was high, many-towered, each tower at this distance
seeming as slender as a racehorse's long legs. The castle
walls were built of a stone that shone pale grey, almost
phosphorescent in the sun's westering light; and as smooth
and faultless as a mirror.

There was the path at the top of the riverbank, paved
as a city street, but the soldier found that he did not want
to take those extra steps away from the river and the
castle and his fortune. All the steps he had taken so far

were toward these things: he would not backtrack now, not even a little. So he took a deep breath and began walking along the grassy edge of the river, over hummocks of weed and grey stones hiding sly moss in their crevices, crushing wild herbs under his heavy boots till their scent was all around him, carrying him forward, pillowing his weary neck and shoulders and easing his tired feet. Thyme and sage he remembered from the stews his mother made, and for a few minutes he was young again; and those few minutes were enough to bring him to the wide low bridge that would lead him over the river to the castle gates.

The bridge was white and handsome, paved with cobblestones. But the stones were round and the foot slid queerly over them, the toe or heel finding itself wedged in a crack between one hump and another, waiting for the other foot to find a place for itself and rescue it, only to begin the uneasy process again. People did not talk much on the bridge, but kept their eyes on their feet, or their hands firmly on the reins and their horses' quarters under them; they could tell well enough where they were by the bridge's gentle arch that rose to meet them and then fell away beneath them till it left them quietly on the far bank. The soldier was accustomed to curious terrain, so he continued to gaze at the castle, although he was aware that his feet were working harder than they had been. At the far end of the bridge the road divided into three; the soldier was the only figure to turn onto the far right-hand way, which led to the castle.

He was on the castle grounds immediately; here was no complex of roads, as in the city, but only the path that he followed, and all around him was the silence of the forest. None hunted here but the King himself with his huntsmen; and the King had lost his pleasure in the chase with the death of his wife, and the animals were nearly tame now. Birds flew overhead, sparrows that dove at him and chirruped, woodcock that whirred straight overhead, pheasants that clacked to each other as they flew; and he caught the gleam of eyes and small furry bodies around the roots and branches of trees. It was hard to believe that any place so green and full of life held any spell as ominous as the one the soldier sought, knowing he would find it; but then, he reflected, why should a spell 'twixt demonkind and human folk, first cousins among creatures, disturb the squirrels and the fish and the deer, who are third cousins at best, and much more sober and responsible about their lives? A young deer, its spots still vaguely discernible on its chestnut-brown back, raised its head from its quiet feeding and peered out at him through the leaves as if reading his mind. "Good day to you," he thought at it, and it lowered its head again. No one but a farmer's son raised on the skirt-edges of the wilderness, or an old campaigner who walked as wild as the game he shared the countryside with, would have seen it at all, enfolded in the forest shadows.

The sun was low when he reached the castle walls, and the iron gates threw bars of shadow first across his path, and then across his face and breast as he approached. The guards who stood at this gate stood no less straight than those he had seen before, but the eyes of these watched him, and when he grew near enough their voices hailed him.

"What business do you seek at the castle of the King?"

The soldier walked on till he stood inside the barred shadow, in the twilight of the courtyard. He replied: "I seek the twelve dancing Princesses, and their father the King; of him I seek the favor of three nights in the Long Gallery, that I may discover where his daughters dance each night."

There was a pause, and the captain of the guard stepped forward: there was gold on the sleeves of his uniform, and his eyes were much like the eyes of the soldier. "You may go if you wish," said the captain, "but I would ask you to stay. I see the Army in the way you walk and answer a hail, and would guess by your eyes that you have come upon hard times. The King's guard can use a man who walks and speaks as you do. Will you not stay here, and leave the Princesses to the nobles' sons, who can do naught else but follow hopeless quests?"

The soldier replied: "I walk as I must, for I bear the wounds of too many battles, and I speak as I must, for I am a farmer's son who learned young to shout at oxen till they moved in the direction one wished; and the nobles' sons do not seem to be following this hopeless quest with a marked degree of success." The cloak of shadows stirred in his knapsack. "I thank you for your offer, for I see your heart in it, but I have had enough of soldiering, and a bad master has ruined me for a good one." But he offered the captain of the guard his hand, and the man took it. "Go then as you will. This road travels straight to the door of the front Hall of the castle, and there, if you will, tell the doorman as you answered the guards' hail; and he will take you to the King. And the King shall receive you with all honor."

"Have there been many recently who walk where I go now?" inquired the soldier.

"No," said the captain of the guard. "There have not been many." And he stepped back into the shadows without saying any more.

The soldier went on up the wide white avenue. Here he heard no birdsong, but the trees seemed to murmur together, high overhead; but perhaps that was only the coming of the night.

At the door of the castle a tall man in a long white robe with a silver belt asked him his business; and the soldier answered as he had answered the guards. And the man bowed to him, which the old soldier found unnerving in a way totally new to him, who was accustomed to awaiting an order to charge the enemy over the next hill, if he hasn't crept round behind while you waited.

The man in white led him inside, into the Great Hall, as the captain of the guard had told him; and the soldier blinked, and realized how dark it had grown outside by the blaze of light that greeted him. A long table ran down the center of the room; and the table was on a dais, and at the end farthest from the soldier was a chair he could recognize as a throne, though he had never seen such a thing before. The man in the white robe bowed to him again, by which he assumed the man meant him to stand where he was; so he waited while the man in white went to the King, and bowed low—much lower than he had to the soldier, as the soldier noted with relief—and spoke to him. And the King himself stood up and came to where the soldier waited, and it took all the soldier's battlefield courage to stand still and not back away as the King, whose health he had toasted and in whose name he had fought many and many a time, strode up to him and looked him in the face.

They were very nearly of a height; the soldier may have had the advantage, or perhaps it was the heavy soles of his boots over the royal slippers. The soldier looked back at the King as the King looked at him; for a moment he wondered if he should bow, but the King's look seemed to wish to forestall him. The soldier saw a face for whom he would be willing to carry colors into battle once more, and the memory of his colonel seemed to fail and fade nearly to oblivion. But it was also a face all those healths drunk and glasses smashed after, to do him honor, had not touched. The sadness of the King's eyes was so deep that it was opaque; nor could the soldier see any small gleam stirring in the depths. The soldier smiled, for pity or for sympathy or for recognition; and did not know he smiled till the King smiled in return; and the King's smile reminded the soldier of something, though he could not quite remember what, and the soldier's smile, for a moment, warmed the King's heart as nothing had done for a very long time. And with the smile suddenly the soldier wondered what the King saw in his face as they looked at one another; but the King did not say, and his smile was only a smile, although it was the smile of a king.

The King said: "Come and eat with us." And he led the way to the high table; and the soldier followed, with his bundle still over his shoulder, and in it he felt the cloak move, like the skin of a horse when a fly touches it. Space was made at the King's right hand, and another chair was brought; and the King sat down in the great chair, and the soldier sat down beside him, and felt his tired bones creak and sigh; and he placed his bundle carefully between his feet, where it curled itself and sat like a cat. And he looked around him as his place was set before him, and counted the other places set; and there were twelve, and twelve chairs before them. Then the white-robed men all stood back, and the Princesses entered.

The soldier would not have been sure that there were twelve of them, had he not counted their chairs before they entered. For each one was more beautiful than the last, in whichever way one counted; and the soldier, who could see an assassin hidden in a tree when the tree was behind him, or notice fear in a new private's face before the private felt it himself, was dazzled by the enchanted Princesses, and nothing he had seen or done or imagined in his life could help him.

The soldier could not remember later if there was any conversation. He remembered that the Princesses moved too slowly for girls as young as they were; even the youngest hovered on the edge of her chair like a chrysalis before the butterfly emerges; barely could the soldier see her eyelashes flicker as she blinked; and her slow fingers only occasionally raised some morsel to her lips. He sat next to the eldest daughter, and he remembered the well woman's words of her, and turned toward her to try to speak, or at least to see something that might guide him; but somehow her face was always turned from him, and he saw only the heavy smoky braids of her hair wound at the nape of her neck; and even if he caught a glimpse of cheekbone or chin, it seemed shadowed, although he could not see where any shadow might fall from: and he thought abruptly that the relentless blaze of light from the many-tiered chandeliers seemed wary, uncertain, as if light was merely the nearest approximation to what actually was sought. The Hall was not lit up for the light, but for the keeping out of the darkness.

The soldier looked across the table to another Princess: she had hair the color of the glossy flanks of the fawn he had seen earlier, and was speckled as it had been too, for she had woven white flowers around her face, and through the delicate crystal crown she wore above her forehead. He caught her eye for a moment, with a trick of the hunter's eye that had seen the fawn: and he saw her eyes widen for a moment as she realized she was caught. He thought she might struggle, as a wild thing would, and he prepared to look away, at a vase, a plate of sweetmeats, because he did not want to see a Princess rearing up like a cornered deer—or worse, cowering away. But to his surprise she met his gaze firmly after that first flicker, and then the tiniest and most wistful of smiles touched her lips and was gone. He looked then at the vase and the sweetmeats but did not see them.

He did not remember what he ate any more than he remembered if there had been conversation. He did remember that men in white robes caught round the waist with belts of bronze and women in silver gowns, their long shining hair caught up in nets like starlight, served him, and the King, and the Princesses, with many dishes; and he thought that he ate a great deal, for he was very hungry and had traveled far on dry bread and hard cheese, and that no one else ate much at all. He also remembered there was music, and music of a complexity, of melodies and drifting harmonies, that described a large number of musicians, and perhaps they played to mask the silence, to distract from the feast that none but the soldier ate, and none enjoyed.

At last the King rose, and with him the Princesses: behind them, on the long high walls of the Great Hall were hung tapestries of all the noble and beautiful and fearful things that had happened to the kings and queens who had lived in the castle for centuries upon centuries past. But nothing in those proud scenes of heroes and ladies and war and mercy was any more noble or fearful than the beauty of the twelve living Princesses who stood before them. The soldier watched the King as he looked at his daughters, each one in turn, and he saw how the sadness of his eyes was so deep that none knew the bottom of it; not even the King himself could reach so far. The soldier knew then the truth of what his friend the ostler had said: that the young noblemen who had had to meet those eyes and say that they had failed could have but little strength or purpose ever after.

Then the Princesses turned; and the youngest leading and the eldest last walked out of the Hall through the door the soldier had entered at, the door they themselves had entered by not long since; and yet, since these twelve passed through it, as light on their feet as hummingbirds resting on the air, so light that it was impossible to imagine their wearing holes in their shoes, be the soles of the thinnest silk: since the Princesses used it as a door the soldier felt suddenly that he must have come in some other, more substantial way. As the dark hair of the eldest, and the last primrose gleam of her gown, disappeared through the door, the soldier thought: "How do I know that she is the eldest? Or that the first of them is the youngest? For none has made me known to any of them. I have never heard their names."

The King turned to him when the door of his daughters' leave-taking was still and empty again, and said to him: "You need not take tonight as your first watch. You have traveled a great distance and deserve a night's untroubled sleep. Tomorrow night is soon enough to begin."

The soldier, standing, as he had stood since the King had risen and the Princesses silently left, felt the lightest of brushes against his ankles, barely a tremor against the heavy leather of his high boots; as if a cat had twitched its tail against him. He heard himself reply: "Sire, I thank you, but your meal has refreshed me enough, and I am anxious to begin the task and trouble your hospitality no further than I must to accomplish it."

The King bowed his head; or at least his eyes dropped from the soldier's face to the white tablecloth.

"One favor I will ask: and that a bath. I fear me travel is a dusty business at best, and I am not the best of travelers."

The King's smile touched his mouth again briefly; and at the raising of his hand, another of the bronze-belted men came up to the two of them, and stood at the foot of the dais so that his head came no higher than their waists, and bowed low, till his white robe swept the floor. "A bath for our guest," said the King. "He then wishes to be brought to the Long Gallery."

The man bowed again, the lesser bow the soldier was coming to recognize, if not resign himself to, as indicating himself; but the man still kept his eyes on the floor so the soldier could catch no glint of his thoughts. Then he turned and slid smoothly away from him, on feet as silent as a hare's; and the soldier stepped awkwardly down from the dais, and followed him, listening to the clumsy thunder of his own boot-soles.

The soldier was appalled by the royal guest bathtub. It was like no indoor bath he had ever seen: it was a lake, and not even the smallest of lakes. As he approached it and looked into the steaming perfumed water, he half expected to see some scaled tropical fish, with fins like battle pennants, peer back at him. But the water was clear to the marble bottom. The steam played delicately with his dusty hair, caressed his cheeks. He closed his eyes a minute. The perfume reminded him of— He opened his eyes again, hurriedly, and began to take off his clothes.

He felt silly, floundering around in an indoor lake—an outdoor one was different, with minnows nipping one's toes, and perhaps a squirrel for company, or a deer come to drink and wonder at the water-monster—and he did not dare stay long in the warm luxurious water, for he had a wakeful night before him. Just a moment he reconsidered the King's offer of a night's grace; regretfully he considered it, and then put it finally aside. He climbed out of the bath and unwound one of the long cream-colored towels that hung on a golden rack shaped like two mermaids holding hands. There were several of these towels, wrapped around the mermaids' necks and lying across their outstretched arms, and the single one he held was big enough to wrap, he thought, all twelve Princesses in.

There was fresh clothing for him in the outer room: a dark red tunic and gold leggings and high soft boots— a soldier's pay in a year's time would not begin to account for the price of one of those boots—and a red cloak with a dark blue collar. He looked at the red cloak, lying in fluid ripples over the back of a silver chair, and then looked around for his bundle. He whirled the red cloak round his shoulder with a gesture, had he known it, that every high-blooded young nobleman had used before him, and picked up his bundle. It sighed at him.

The servant—if it was the same one: they were all white-robed and brown-haired and somber—appeared at the door as if he had waited for the chink of a belt-buckle as a summons to enter. That belt the soldier had found under the red cloak: the tails of two green dragons wound together at the small of his back, and their golden fangs locked in front. Their sapphire eyes glittered at him as he looked down at them. The bundle, hung idly over his wrist when he grasped the belt, shivered with impatience; and the serving man stepped through the door.

The soldier looked up and nodded; the man never quite met his eyes, but bowed his bow and turned again and left the room, and the soldier followed, his footfalls now as silent as the servant's. This man led the way down a long corridor and up a flight of stairs that blazed with light as the Great Hall had; but at the top of these stairs the light abruptly ended. The servant seized a candelabrum from a niche at the stairhead and raised it high with a hand that did not tremble, and the light's rays flew down the corridor as swift and straight as hawks. To the left was a plain wall, running from the stairhead to the end of the corridor, which was blind but for a tiny barred window a hand's-breadth above man-level. "No escape that way," thought the old campaigner's part of the soldier's mind. He looked left, at the wall: in it was set one door, only two steps from the head of the stairs where they stood. It was a door tall and broad, seven feet high perhaps and four wide, and bound with iron. There was no gap or break or fissure in it anywhere but for a keyhole so heavily wound around with iron that the opening seemed no thicker than a needle. From the keyhole a flake of white light shone from inside the door.

He looked to his right: here the wall was pierced by a series of arched windows, their lower edges at waist level, where one might rest elbows and gaze out, if one ever wished to linger in this weary spot. "But perhaps the view from these windows is very fine by day," thought the soldier. "You can see what is coming up the river at you," thought the campaigner. But now the windows were muffled in the shadows of a cloudy night. No star glittered; the very air seemed grey beyond the casement glass. "And," thought the soldier, "the air must always seem grey in this place from the shadow of the iron-barred door of the Long Gallery, which looms behind you on the brightest of summer mornings."

One of the shadows now moved and became the King; and the soldier realized that he had expected him to be here before himself. Something dark hung against his breast: as he came into the candlelight that swooped to touch the end of the hall but left the clouded windows to themselves, the soldier saw that at the center of the

royal silken robes hung a small iron key. Its very refusal
to glitter or shine made it catch the eye.

The King lifted the thin chain from around his neck,
and slowly fitted the key into the lock. The light-flake
disappeared; and then with a gentle *chunk* the lock
turned, the door began to open, and an edge of light
appeared instead around its frame. The servant stepped
back, the soldier's instincts, rather than his eyes or ears,
told him; then in the background the shadows moved, and
as the door swung fully open, the man set the candelabrum back in its niche and retreated down the stairs.

The light seemed too white and pure for candlelight,
as it flooded out and swept around the soldier and the
King; but perhaps this was due to the snowiness of the
linen it reflected. Twelve white-hung beds stood, their
heads to the far wall, in a long line down the Gallery;
and six Princesses in long white nightgowns with fragile
lace at the wrists and throats sat on the counterpanes, or
on stools, and had their hair brushed by their white-
gowned sisters. No one spoke: the air was stirred only by
the soft crackle of comb-teeth and fingers through long
sleek hair. The soldier thought confusedly of barracks; and
then he blushed like a boy at his first dance, and his feet
would not cross the threshold. He could not do what he
had come so far to try; it was not right, and what he had
heard could not be. He looked at the warm gleam of their
foreheads and cheeks, the gentle rise and fall of the white
nightgowns as they breathed, and watched the murmur
of the light in the waves of hair, and was certain that it
was all the most terrible of mistakes. These girls were
not haunted. They were too beautiful and too serene.

Too calm. He remembered the youngest Princess at the banquet none enjoyed; and then her father stepped around him till he could look in his eyes, and waved him across the doorsill. This time his feet agreed, if reluctantly, to take him forward. Perhaps he heard, or perhaps he imagined, the King whispering, "Godspeed"; and then he did hear the door close behind him. For a moment even the hands twisting the heavy falls of hair were still, so the closing of the door spoke in perfect silence. The soldier heard no sound at all of the turning of the key; but he was no less certain that the key had turned, bolting him and twelve Princesses into the Gallery for the night. His pulse pounded so it threatened to obscure his sight as well as his hearing. Perhaps the Princesses' young ears caught a sound his cannon-hardened ones could not: for as he was thinking all this, and feeling his heart beating in his throat, twelve Princesses sighed and bowed their heads, and stared at white laps and white hands for a moment, and then took up again the movements the King and the soldier had interrupted so recently.

Several turned their eyes slowly toward the soldier; their faces were without expression as they gazed at him, but with an expressionlessness that he did not like. The eyes glittered like the eyes behind masks. If they had been men, he would be watching their hands, waiting for the quick hard appearance of hidden knives: and then he did look at the hands of the Princess nearest him, and saw them clenched in her lap. The pale purity of her skin was pulled taut and unhappy across the frail knuckles; and his own face softened. When he looked at their faces again, the expressionlessness now seemed that of a burden almost too heavy to bear, and the glitter in their eyes that of unshed tears.

Then the Princess he remembered, who had sat across from him at dinner, approached him; and he saw the same wistful smile hesitantly curl her lips and drop away again at once. He followed her to the end of the Gallery, listening to the slightest rustle of her long white skirts; and he noticed suddenly and with a shock he could not explain that her feet were bare.

There was a screen set up in the farthest corner, next to the windowless end of the long chamber. Behind it, next to the narrow wall, was a low cot, with blankets and pillows. The Princess gestured toward it, bowed her head to him briefly, and left him. He turned to catch a glimpse of her bare heels as she vanished beyond the screen.

He sat heavily down and stared at his feet in their fine boots. His bundle lay on the cot beside him and rested against his knee. He found himself thinking of his age, turning the years over, one by one, in his mind, like the leaves of a book. His eyes slowly focused on a lamp that stood by the screen on a little three-legged table, with a tinder-box beside it; but he made no move toward it.

He looked up to see the eldest Princess framed by the light that flowed around the edge of the screen. He could not see her face, but he was sure it was she, as he had recognized her as she sat beside him at dinner. He wondered if his silent understanding of these Princesses was true; and if it was, was it an omen for good or ill? The Princess held a goblet in her hand; her arm was held out in a graceful curve, and the white sleeve fell back to reveal her slim forearm. She held the goblet high, as if it were a victory chalice, and the soldier was reminded of old statues he had seen, of the goddess of war: thus she might carry the severed head of the conquered hero, beautifully and pitilessly. The Princess offered him the goblet, and he took it, and found it surprisingly heavy. "Drink, and be welcome," she said, but there was no warmth or greeting in her voice.

He raised the goblet to his lips, but turned his head as he did, so she might see only his profile; and he poured the sweet-smelling wine gently down his back, and he felt the red cloak sag with it. "I thank thee, lady," he said, "for wine and welcome."

She bowed her head as her sister had done, but for the space of a minute or more; then she straightened herself abruptly, with a gesture he recognized from battlefields he and his fellows had won their weary way across, and left him without another word.

He sat looking after her for a moment, and then reached up to unfasten the dark red cloak. It was warm and wet to his fingers as he pulled it off; it came heavily now, sodden as it was, with none of the brisk furl and unfurl it had greeted him with when he picked it up first. He dropped it on the floor beside his cot; it steamed with the drugged wine, and he blinked as the clouds of it rose to his eyes.

He listened. The blood no longer pounded in his ears. The blaze of light from around the edge of the screen continued unwavering; and the silence was perfect. It waited. He wondered for what: and then he knew. So he sighed, and moved on the cot till it creaked; and as he did this, he opened his bundle, and lifted out the night-colored cloak the woman at the well had given him. He lay heavily down, full-length, on the cot, and noisily rearranged the linen-clad pillows with one hand; he held the cloak in the other, and it wrapped softly around his wrist and up his arm. Then he sighed once more, and lay still, crossing his hands on his breast. The cloak wandered over his shoulders and brushed his throat.

The silence still waited. The soldier snored once. Twice. A third time.

Then the rustling began: the sound of hasty bare feet, of skirts, of chest-lids almost silent but not quite; then of silks and satins and brocades, tossing together, murmuring over each other, jostling and sighing and whirling. And the sounds of bare feet were no more; instead the soldier, between snores, heard the sounds of the soles of exquisite little shoes: dancing shoes, made for princesses' feet; and he knew that only haste, that caused even princesses to be careless of how they set their feet, enabled him to hear them at all. Then the soldier, with a last snore, stood up as softly as many years of the most dangerous of scouting missions had taught him, and whisked the black cloak around his shoulders. It blew like a shadow around him and settled without weight. Then he heard a laugh, low and brief, as if cut off, and not a happy laugh; a laugh from a heart that has not laughed for pleasure in a long time. It was the only voice he heard. He stepped around the screen.

The twelve Princesses huddled at the opposite end of the Long Gallery; and he walked toward them, softly as a scout in the enemy's camp, softly as a fox in the

chicken coop, softer still for what haunted things with
quick ears might be listening. He heard a sound again
like the lifting of a chest-lid; but this must be a massive
chest, with a great lid. The Princesses all stood back and
gazed toward the floor: there a great hatch had been
uncovered, at the foot of the farthest bed, and beside it
the eldest Princess knelt, with her hands at the edge of
the trapdoor she had just raised. She stared downward
with her sisters. The Princesses were all dressed in the
loveliest of gowns; they shimmered like bubbles caught
in the sun's rays, that look clear as glass, but with every
color finely in and through and over them, till the eye
is dazzled. Like some faerie bubble the eldest Princess
seemed as she rose to her feet and floated—down. Each of
her sisters followed lightly after; and as the last bit of
the rainbow skirt of the youngest disappeared through
the trap, the soldier stepped down the dark stair behind
her.

It was dark for only a moment. There was a light
coming mistily from somewhere before them toward
which they descended. It made its way a little even into
the long black flight of stairs that sank below the King's
castle. The walls that clung close around those stairs were
moist to the touch, as if they walked by the river. Down
they went, and still farther down; the grey light grew
a little stronger and the sullen air no longer felt like a
cloud in the lungs. The soldier blinked, and looked at
his feet, or where his feet should be, for he had forgotten
his cloak; and at that he stumbled—and stepped on the
hem of the youngest Princess's dress. A tiny breathless

shriek leaped from her, and she clutched at the glittering necklaces at her throat.

Her sisters paused and looked back at her, and the soldier recognized the same voice that had earlier laughed so mirthlessly. "Someone just stepped on the hem of my dress," she said, trembling, but her hands still clutched at her jewels, and she did not, or could not, look behind her.

"Don't be absurd," said the eldest; her voice drifted back along the shadowy corridor, touching the walls, like a bird so long imprisoned it no longer seeks to be free, but flies only because it has wings. "That soldier drank the wine I gave him; you heard him snoring. You have caught your skirt on a nail."

The soldier leaned against a dank wall, his heart pounding till he thought the fever-quick perceptions of the youngest Princess must hear it; but as her eleven sisters began their descent again she followed after, with only the briefest hesitation. One small hand clutched at her skirt, and pulled the edge up, so that it would not trail behind her; and she hurried to walk close at the heels of the eleventh Princess, as if she feared to linger; but not once did she look behind her.

Still they descended; but the dark walls rose up till the soldier could no longer see the ceiling; and these heavy brooding walls were now pierced with arches, and within the arches there were things that shimmered, red and green and blue and gold. The soldier peered into them as he passed; and then suddenly the walls fell away entirely, and still they descended, but the stairs were cut into what appeared to be a cliff of stone, black, with veins of silver and green; and the thin shining lines seemed to stir like snakes. And lining the stairs on either side were trees: but the trees were smooth and white, with a white that was frightening, for it was a white that did not know the sun; and in the strange branches of these strange trees, if trees they even could be called, grew gems, as huge and heavy as ripe plums and peaches. The soldier paused and thought: "A branch of a tree will help me tell my story to the King," and he put a hand out, quickly, so his fingers touched the cool white bole before he was overcome again by the vertigo of not being able to see himself; and so his hand closed around a branch, and he did not fall. He let his fingers creep blindly to a twig's end, and broke off a spray of young gems, delicate as rosebuds and no larger than the fingertips of the youngest Princess; but these rosebuds were purple and blue and the shifting greens of hidden mosses.

The crack of the breaking branch echoed terribly in that vast underground chamber; and again the youngest Princess shrieked, a high, thin, desperate sound. But this time she whirled around, her hands in fists, and her fists against her mouth, holding in the weeping. Her eyes stared back up, and up, the way they had come, and the soldier stood motionless, although he knew she could not see him. He held the branch as he had broken it, as if it still were a part of the tree; and he looked at the youngest Princess's wide wild eyes, and he felt pity for her.

Then the eldest came back to her, and put an arm round her, and whispered to her, but the soldier could not hear what she said. But her little sister slumped, and rested her head against the elder's shoulder, and they stood so a moment. Then the youngest straightened up and dropped her hands, and they turned back to the other ten of their sisters, who were still looking up the long stair. "We will go on now," the eldest said, like a general to his tired army.

The soldier slipped the branch under his cloak and followed. The cloak clung to his shoulders as if by its own volition; but he no longer heard its whispering, and it held to him closely, motionless, not as any other cloak would sway and swing to his own motion.

The soldier now turned his eyes back to the eldest Princess as she descended the stairs in small running steps; her sisters turned round as she passed them, but none stirred from their places till she was again at the bottom of the luminous rainbow line of them. And now the soldier saw that the stair was almost ended, and before them was a wide black lake: so wide he could not see to its far bank. He blinked, as if his eyes were somehow at fault; but they were used to the light of the upper earth, of sun and moon and stars, and they were unhappy and uncertain here. He squinted up toward the—ceiling? It was a dull green, like a pool that has lain in its bed too long undisturbed. As a ceiling, it was high and vast; as a sky, it was heavy and watchful. The soldier's shoulders moved as if they felt the weight of it, and the cloak of shadows was wrapped around him almost as if it were afraid.

He let his feet take him gently down the last stairs; they were broad and low and smooth now, and any treachery they carried was not in their shape. As he reached the shore of the black lake he saw there were boats on the water, boats as black as the ripples they threw out, and at their sterns stood men with poles. He listened to the sound of the ripples as they lapped against the shore; and they sounded like no water he had ever heard before.

The eldest Princess stepped forward, head high; and she took the outstretched hand of the steersman of the first boat, and stepped lightly into it. The soldier, watching, thought the rails did not dip with her weight, nor the small boat settle any deeper in the water. And he still listened to the small claws of the bow-waves walking on the shore. The second, then third Princesses mounted the second and third boats, and the soldier noticed that there were twelve of the black skiffs, and twelve men to pole them; and each man wore a black cape, and a black wide-brimmed hat with a curling feather; but the black-gloved hands held out to the princesses sparkled with jewels.

The soldier stood beside the youngest Princess, and stepped in as she did; and the boat dipped heavily. The Princess turned pale behind her bright-painted cheeks, but the soldier could not see the man's face. He poled the boat around swiftly and with an ease that the soldier read as many nights' experience of the Princesses' mysterious dancing. There was no room for the soldier in the little boat; when the Princess had settled, gracefully if uneasily, in the bow, he stood amidships, his soft-soled boots pressed against the boat's curving ribs. The small waves on the boat's skin sounded with a thinner keen than they had on the shore.

"We go slowly tonight," said the youngest Princess nervously, turning her head to look at the eleven other boats fanned out before them. The gap between them and the next-to-last boat was widening. The soldier had his back to the man, who after a moment replied: "I do not know how it is, but the boat goes heavily tonight."

The Princess turned her head again and gazed straight at the soldier: it seemed she met his eyes. He stared back at her, unblinking, as if they were conspirators; but she took her eyes away without recognition. The soldier found he had to unclench his fists after she looked away. He breathed shallowly, and tried to time his breathing to the slow sweep of the pole, that if it were heard at all, it would sound only as part of the black water's echo.

The man said: "Do not fear. There will still be enough dancing for you even if we arrive behind the others by a little."

The Princess turned back to stare ahead, and did not speak again.

The soldier made out fitful gleams across the water: lights shining out against the dull toad-colored air. As they approached nearer, the soldier could make out the shore that was their destination; and it was blazing with lights, lanterns the size of a man's body set on thick columns barely an arm's length one from another. The soldier thought of the banqueting hall where he had dined but a few hours ago, but he stopped his thoughts there, and turned them to another road. He saw that it was not the opposite shore they approached, but a pier; and the eleven other boats were tied there already, and their passengers gone. The boats moved quietly together

on the water, empty, as if they were holding a sly conversation. The soldier looked left and right, and saw the
dark water stretching away from him, breaking up the
chips of light from the lanterns into smaller chips, and
tossing them from wave to wave, and swallowing them
as quickly as they might, and greedily reaching for more.
He wondered if the pier was on no shore at all, but built
out from an island raised up out of the waters after some
fashion no mortal could say. Then he looked forward
again, beyond the lights, and saw the castle, and many
graceful figures moving within it; and through its wide
gates he could see eleven rainbow figures, a little apart
from the rest still, turning and lightly turning, moving
across the lights behind them, disappearing for a moment
behind the pier lights that dazzled the soldier's eyes, and
as lightly reappearing: dancing. And each of them seemed
to be dancing opposite a shadow, whose arms round their
waists seemed like iron chains, breaking their slender
radiance into two pieces.

Then the boat touched the pier, and the last Princess
leaped out, as silent as a fawn, and the soldier followed
slowly. The white castle reared up like a dream out of
the darkness, hemmed around by the great lanterns that
seemed to lift up their light to it like homage. The Princess stood as if standing still were the most difficult thing
she had ever known; and then a man stood beside her.
The soldier thought he must be the same man who had
poled the boat; but he had thrown his cape and over-
shadowing hat aside, and the soldier, who had never had
any particular thought of a man's beauty, was shaken by
the sight of this man's face. He smiled upon the Princess

a smile that she should have treasured for years; but she only looked back at him and held up her arms like a child who wishes to be picked up. The man closed his black-sleeved arms gently about her, and then they were dancing, dancing down the pier, and across the brilliantly lit courtyard and through the shining gates, till they joined the rest of the beautiful dancers, and the soldier could no longer tell one couple from the next. He could tell the walls of the castle, he felt, only because they stood still; for there was a grace and loveliness to them that seemed too warm for stone: warm enough for breath and life. And now as he looked back within the castle gates he realized he could pick out his twelve Princesses by the pale luminescence of their gowns against the black garb of their partners; but this time the soldier admired them longingly and humbly, for he saw the perfect pairs they made, like night and day. And the twelve couples wove in and out of a vividly dressed, dancing throng, brilliant with all colors.

He stood where he had first stepped out of the boat, and felt as he stood that his legs would snap if he moved them; then they began to tremble, and he sat heavily down, and leaned against one of the lantern pillars, and for the first time he wondered why he had come, why he should wish to break the enchantment that held the Princesses captive. Captive? The magnificence of this castle was far greater than the simple splendor that the Princesses' father owned. He looked up from the foot of his pillar. He could not see the low green sky against the lanterns' brilliance, and such was the power of this place he was now in that he almost wondered if he had imagined it; this palace could not exist beneath that sight-less sky.

His eyes went back to the tall castle, smooth as opal, with the flashing figures passing before its wide doors, and the light flooding over all. He thought again of the un-earthly beauty of the man who had danced with the youngest Princess, and knew without thinking that the other eleven were as handsome. He remembered the weary old woman at the well, the shabbiness of her hut and her gown—how could she know the truth of what she said? She could never have seen this place.

The soldier shut his eyes. Then for the first time he heard the music, as if hitherto his mind had been too dazzled by what his eyes saw; but now the music glided to him and around him, to tell him even more about the wonder of this island in a black lake. This music was as if the sweetest notes of the sweetest instruments ever played were gathered together for this one orchestra, for this single miraculous castle at the heart of an endless black sea.

He bowed his head to his knees and sighed; and the cloak of shadows loosened a little from his shoulders and crept over his arms and neck as if to comfort him. Then he felt an irregular hardness against his chest and remem-bered the branch of the jewel tree. He drew it out and gazed at it, turning it this way and that in the abundant white light; and it sparkled at him, but told him nothing. He put it away again and felt old, old.

"And if I do this thing," he thought suddenly, "not only will they never see this castle of heart's delight again, nor their handsome lovers; but—one of them must marry me.

"Not the youngest," he thought. "At least not the youngest."

He tried to remember seeing her in her father's hall, to remember the feeling he had had then of an unnatural quietness in her, in her sisters: and he thought, indeed it was a hard thing to live by day on earth, when the mind is full of the splendors of this place; splendors only seen the night before and in the night to come. Soon, the old woman had said, soon the Princesses would open their father's world to this one, and dwell freely in both, forever, with their bright-faced princes. Soon.

The soldier had no idea how long he sat thus, back against a lantern post, knees drawn up and head bowed. But he stirred at last, looked up, stood; faced the castle as if he would walk into it boldly. But as he looked through the gates, he saw several of the dancing pairs halt: not the ones wearing greens and blues and reds, but the ones brilliant in black and white, moonlight and darkness. Three of them; then four—six, seven, nine. Twelve. Other dancers whirled by, careless of any who must stop, and the music continued, eerie and marvelous, without pause or hesitation. But twelve couples slowly separated themselves from the crowd and made their way toward the pier where twelve black skiffs and a sad and weary soldier waited.

The soldier stepped into the last skiff with the youngest Princess as he had done before; and again he stood amidships and stared out over the bow. But his thoughts lay in the bottom of his mind without motion, and he saw little that his eyes rested on. Occasionally he touched the branch of the jewel tree with his fingers as if it were some charm, some reality in this land of green sky: the reality of a world whose trees budded gems.

The black boats grounded softly on the lake shore, their wakes scratching at the land. The soldier stepped out and followed the Princesses up the long stair. He did not turn back to catch any last glimpse of the black boats and their shadowed captains: nor did any of the Princesses. He saw instead, as he looked ahead of him, an occasional dainty foot beneath its skirt, leaving a step behind to reach a step above: and in a quick flash of delicate soles he could see the slippers were worn through, till the pink skin showed beneath.

The heavy trapdoor at the end of the stair still stood open, and a blaze of candles greeted them as they drew near, though the tall candles they had left were now near guttering. The soldier wondered that his breath slid in and out of his breast so easily, after bending and straightening his stiff legs up so many stairs: and thought perhaps it was but more of the enchantment of the land of green sky, of gemmed trees and black water, and a white castle upon an island.

The soldier slipped through the Princesses who stood around the hatch in the Long Gallery, gazing down for one last look at the land they lived in each night, before the eldest Princess knelt and closed it. The door fell shut like a coffin-lid, with the same rough whisper it spoke upon opening. The soldier made his way down the Long Gallery to his screen and his cot; and he pulled off the cloak of shadows, which sighed and then went limp in his hands as if it too were sad and exhausted. He lay down silently upon his cot, the cloak bundled beneath his ear, the jeweled branch protected by the breast of his tunic, and he turned his back to the Princesses' Gallery and faced the blind wall, so that any that might choose to spy upon their spy could not notice the curious bulge it made.

And he felt, rather than saw, that the eldest Princess came and looked upon him. He could feel the shadow of her lying gracefully across his legs, and feel the silence of her face, the sweep of her glance. Then she went away, as straight and proud as he had seen her when she brought him the wine.

PART TWO

THE SOLDIER awoke late that morning as though he were climbing out of a pit, hand over hand. He was stiff, as with battle, but the stiffness was not so much that of the muscles as of the mind: the reluctance to rise and look upon yesterday's battlefield, though you bore no mark yourself; to look upon the faces of those who had been your friends and had been killed, and upon those belonging to the other side, whom you and your friends had killed. And upon those of that other army who returned in the morning as you were doing, to bury their dead, their living faces as stiff as your own.

But the soldier, lying in his cot at the end of the Long Gallery, with his night cloak under his ear, awoke to a terrible sense of not knowing where he was. Having clambered up and out of the pit of sleep, he peered over the edge, blinking, and did not recognize what he saw.

For all his long years in the Army the soldier had depended on his ability to awaken instantly, to leap in the right direction if need be to save his life, before his eyelids were quite risen, before his waking mind was called upon to consider and decide. In the moment that it took for the soldier to feel the sharp points of the gem-tree at his breast, to recognize the blind stone wall before his eyes, he lay chill with a horror that was infinite, lying as still as a deer in its bed of brush, not knowing where the hunter stood but sure that he was there, waiting. When memory swept back to him he breathed once, twice, deeply and deliberately, and slowly sat up; and he thought: "I left the regiment just in time. I am too old indeed to live as a hunted thing, hunted and hunter." He looked down at the cloak of shadows that lay curled over the pillow, and a second thought walked hard on the heels of the first: "But what adventure is this that I have exchanged for my own peace?" For suddenly it appeared to him that his life in the regiment had at least been one of simple things, and things that permitted hope; and the path he walked now was dark and unknowable.

The Long Gallery was empty and the heavy door the King had locked the night before stood open. The soldier paused to wrap the jeweled branch in a blanket from his cot; then he threw the wine-stained cloak over his shoulder in a manner such that one could not see the bundle he carried under his arm; and he walked swiftly out. Suddenly he wanted no more than to stand outside the haunted castle with its haunted chamber, and look upon the world of trees that bore green leaves and blue sky, and hear the birds sing. He remembered that birds did sing in the deep forests around the King's castle; and he thought perhaps this was a thing he could take hope from.

He made his way as quickly as he might down the

stairs to the great front doors of the castle, and through them he went without pausing. He saw no one, nor did any challenge him, as he walked through the King's house and into his lands as if he had the right to use them so.

The day was high, clear and cloudless, and the world was wide as he stood looking around him. He could taste the air in his mouth, and the memory of the night before was washed away like brittle ashes from a hearth when a bucket of clean water is tossed over it. He walked on, the bundle still held close under his arm: and his steps took him at last, without his meaning them to, to the guardhouse; and there the captain was the man the soldier had spoken to the evening before; and the captain came out of the guardhouse as the soldier neared, but he said no word.

"I have come to ask a favor," said the soldier, for he had thought, as he saw the captain's face again, of the favor that this man might do him.

"Name it," said the captain. "We are comrades after all, for each of us walks at the edge of a dangerous border, and makes believe that he is the guardian of it."

The soldier bowed his head and brought out the blanket-wrapped bundle. "Can you keep this safe for me? Safe from any man's eyes, or anyone's knowledge?"

The captain's eyes flickered at *anyone*. "I will keep it as safe as mortal man may," he replied. "I have the way of no more."

A bit of a smile twisted one corner of the soldier's mouth. "Nor have I," said the soldier. "As one mortal man to another, I thank you."

Another wandering piece of a smile curled around the captain's mouth, and the soldier held the bundle out to him, and the captain took it. "Good hunting to you, comrade," he said.

"Thank you," said the soldier, but the smile had disappeared. He turned away and off the path, and walked into the forest.

He walked a long time, breathing the air and rubbing leaves between his fingers that he might catch the sharp fresh scent of them; and he went so quietly, or they were so tame, that he saw deer, does and bucks and spotted fawns, and rabbits brown and grey, a fox, and a marten which clung to the branch of a tree and looked down at him with black inscrutable eyes. Birds there were, many of them: those that croaked or rasped a warning of his coming or going, those that darted across clearings or from bush to bush before him; those that sat high in the branches of the trees and sang for or despite him; and those that wheeled silently overhead.

In the late afternoon he sat on the bank of the river and watched the sun go down and reluctantly admitted to himself that he was hungry, for he had had nothing to eat that day but the fruit he had pulled from the trees of the King's orchard. But it was with a heavy foot nonetheless that he took the first step back to the castle.

A servant stood by the door at his entrance, and he was escorted directly upstairs to the bath-room, where the deep steaming pool again awaited him, and fresh clothes were laid out in the dressing-room. He washed and dressed, and then he picked up the wine-stained cloak of the night before and looked at it thoughtfully.

He carried it back into the bath-room and looked around. A ewer of fresh water stood near the massive bathtub, and the soldier dropped the cloak into it. He dropped to his knees beside it—like any washerwoman, he thought wryly—and swished the cloak clumsily around in the water. He could smell, faint but clear, the odor of the wine lifting out of the ewer. He brought soap from the bath, and scrubbed and wrung and scrubbed the cloak till his knuckles were sore and his opinion of washer-women had risen considerably; and then he rinsed the draggled cloak in another water urn, and hung the sodden mass over the edge of the tub where it might drip without harming the deep carpet that lay in front of the door to the dressing-room. "I've ruined it, no doubt," he thought. "Well, let them wonder." And he picked up the fresh cloak that was laid out with his other new clothes, and turned and went downstairs to the banquet.

The banquet was as it had been the evening before: magnificent with its food and the beauty of the Princesses and the splendor of their clothes—and he observed this evening with interest that the clothes they wore were of ordinary, if rich, hues; their rainbow gowns did not appear in their father's hall—and oppressive with a silence that hung in the ear like a threat, and was not muffled by the music of the King's elegant musicians. The soldier ate, for he was hungry; but he barely recognized his own hand, the wrist and forearm draped in a sleeve too gaudy to be that of an old soldier too weary for war, and the food in his mouth was as tasteless as wood chips. And the blaze of the candelabra hurt his eyes.

He dreaded the night ahead; but for all that, he was

relieved when the banquet that was no banquet was finished; and he stood at the King's side as the Princesses went their way from the hall, one after another, heads high, their jewels shining, their eyes shadowed. The soldier stared at the eldest as she walked toward the door at the end of the procession; and she turned her face a little away from him as if she were aware of his look. "No," he thought. "If she turns from anyone's gaze, it is from her father's."

When the last Princess was gone, the King turned to his guest, and the soldier read the helpless, hopeless question in the father's eyes. But the soldier remembered sitting on a pier, leaning against a post, and watching a dance in a hall so grand as to make this castle look a cotter's hut; and the soldier's eyes dropped. Another man in the King's place might have sighed, have touched his face with his hand, have made some sign. But the King did not. When the soldier glanced up at him again he saw a face so still that it might have been a statue's, cold and perfect and lifeless, and the soldier looked at the straight brow, the long nose, and the wide mouth; a mouth that had once known well how to smile and laugh, but had now nearly forgotten; and the lines of laughter in that face hurt the heart of any who recognized them for what they were. And the soldier thought again of the ostler's tale.

Then the King's eyes blinked, and were no longer staring at something the soldier would not see even if he turned around and looked into the bright shadowless corner the King had looked into; and he began to breathe again, lightly, easily, and the soldier realized that the

King had drawn no breath since the soldier had first dropped his eyes before the King's unanswered question.

The King turned and led the way from the Hall, and they went up the stairs to the grim hall off which the Gallery opened through one thick ungraceful door. The two of them, weary King and weary soldier, leaned their elbows on the balustrade and stared into the night; this evening the sky glittered with stars as bright as hope. A single servant stood at the head of the stairs, who had followed the King softly when he first left the dining hall; and the servant held a candelabrum of only three candles. Their light brushed hesitantly at the darkness of the corridor.

The King turned at last and took the iron key on its chain from around his neck, and pulled open the door to the Long Gallery. The soldier entered and stood, his eyes upon the toes of his boots; and this night as he stood he heard with the twelve listening Princesses the sound of the door swung shut behind him, a tiny pause, and then the snick of the lock run home.

The evening passed much as had the evening before. The soldier, his eyes still lowered, made his way down the long chamber, past twelve silent white-gowned Princesses, to his dark narrow cot behind the screen. There he sat, thinking of nothing, staring at the unlit lamp, the cloak of shadows beneath his hand and another handsome cloak, this one of deep blue, over his shoulders. The eldest Princess came to him again, and offered him wine to drink; and they exchanged words, but the words left no mark upon the soldier's memory. He poured the hot wine, gently and carefully, into the folds of his handsome blue cloak; and even the heavy spiced steam of the drink seemed to make his eyelids droop, his head nod. And he was sharply aware of the Princess's glance, and kept his mouth firmly closed, as if he were afraid that his hand, under her look, might somehow stray and bring the wine to his lips against his will. And he wondered at what it might be that directed her hand when she drugged the wine, what peered through her eyes as she gave it to the mortal watcher waiting behind the screen. He handed the empty goblet to the tall waiting figure, and she left him silently.

He lay down and began to snore, but with pauses between the snores, that he might hear the sound of the heavy door being opened, the door that led to the underground kingdom. He snored still as he rose, and tossed the black cloak around him, in place of the wine-heavy blue one that lay in its turn on the floor beside the cot; and then he stopped snoring, and slipped around the edge of his screen, and saw the twelfth Princess watching the tail of the eleventh's dress gliding through the hatch. Then she too descended, and the soldier cautiously followed.

Nothing marred their descent this night; for the soldier knew what he would find, and he made no mistakes. He looked at the jeweled trees as he passed them, but he did not touch them; their purpose was served. Tonight he must seek something further.

The twelve black boats waited by the shore of the black lake; the water's edge, clawing at the pebbles, seemed almost to speak to him; but he dared not listen too long. Tonight the oarsman in the twelfth boat must have put more strength in his labor, for despite the soldier's invisible presence athwartships, staring toward the glittering island he knew would be there, the last boat kept near the others, and docked with them. The soldier set his jaw, and leaped ashore behind the Princess, as the black captain held the boat delicately touching the pier; and he watched as the captains of all the twelve boats whirled out of their long black cloaks and wide-brimmed hats and stood at the princesses' sides, as fearfully handsome as the Princesses were beautiful. But the soldier clutched his black cloak to him all the closer, and was curiously grateful for the way it clutched back. And as the gleaming pairs of dancers swept from dockside into the arms of the music that reached out from the castle's opened gates, the soldier followed after them, walking slowly but without hesitation.

There were many others within the broad ballrooms of that castle besides the Princesses and their partners; he had not realized, the night before, even as he was dazzled and bewildered by the bright colors they wore and the intricate dance steps they pursued, just how many others were present. The music thrummed in the soldier's ears and beat against his invisible skin till he felt that anyone looking at him must see the outline that the melodies and counterpoints drew around him.

But none appeared to suspect his presence, and he walked boldly through the high rooms, and blinked at the light and the glitter. The rooms seemed as intensely lit as the banqueting hall of the Princesses' father, and he found the glare here no less disquieting to his mind, and much

more so to his eyes, which were dazzled by twelves upon
twelves upon twelves upon twelves of dancing figures,
all glorying in gold and silver and gems, not only in head-
dresses and necklaces, rings, brooches and bracelets, but
wrought into their clothing; even fingernails and eyelids in
this enchanted place gleamed like diamonds; and none was
ever still. He found he could think of the unnatural stillness of the Princesses in their father's home as restful,
soothing, something to remember with pleasure and relief
rather than bewilderment.

The soldier had no sense of time. He wove through the
crowds and stared around him; he felt confused by the
light and the brilliant music; he remembered his thoughts
of the night before, huddled against a dockside post, and
he shivered, and his cloak pressed tighter around his
throat. But he reached out to steady himself, one hand
upon the gorgeous scrolls of an ivory-inlaid doorframe;
and for a moment, with that touch, his mind seemed clear
and calm, suspended behind his eyes where it might
watch and consider what went on around him, without
feeling the fears that thundered unintelligibly at him. And
he saw, then, something beyond the scintillation of gems
and precious things beyond counting, beyond the ele-
gance, the grace and sheer overwhelming beauty of the
scene before him. He saw that the faces of the throng were
blank and changeless, the lightness of step, of gesture,
the perfections of automatons. None spoke; the splendor
of the constant music did but disguise the unnatural silence of the many guests; again the soldier thought of the
King's musicians playing gallantly to hide the silence of
their master and his daughters. Yet there one listened to

the music because one could hear the sorrow behind it that it sought to conceal, even to soften. Here, to listen carefully to what lay behind the music was to court madness, for what lay beyond it was the emptiness of the void. The soldier thought of his own shabby clumsiness, but now suddenly he had some respect for it, because it was human.

And as he thought these things, clear, each of them, as such a sky as he had seen over the surface of his beloved earth only yesterday afternoon, he saw the eldest Princess stepping toward him, one white hand laid quietly on the arm of her tall black-haired escort. The two of them together made such a beautiful sight his heart ached within him for all his new sunlit wisdom; but he looked at them straight, staring the longest at the Princess. He felt then that to stare at her, to memorize each line of her face, each hollow and shadow and curve, would be a comfort and a relief to him; and if the woman at the well was correct—and tonight the hope had returned that she might be—the Princess would not begrudge it him. And so he looked at her, and as he looked the ache in his heart changed: for he saw that her chin was raised just a little too high, and she placed each slim foot just a little too carefully. The expressionlessness on her face was as flawless as her beauty, but he thought he knew, now, what it was costing her. The two of them walked by him, unknowing; he turned his head to watch them go. They left the great halls of the palace; he saw them fade into the shadows of blackness beyond the courtyard till the blaze of the torches at the portals blinded him and he could not tell them from the gems on the Princess's gown.

And so the second night wore to its end, and the soldier

followed the Princesses home to the Long Gallery, and heard the stone hatch sigh closed. He lay on his bed and snored; and rose the next morning and looked around him, and remembered the night before, and the night before that one. And so he recalled that tonight was his third and last night to share the Princesses' chamber, and discover their secret if he would, as so many had tried before. And he knew that as he sat this morning blinking at his boots, so tomorrow morning would a messenger await him at the iron-bound door to the Princesses' Gallery, to lead him before them, and before the King, and to account for the boon the King had granted him.

So on the third night the soldier looked around him with the eyes of one who seeks some exact thing when he strode into the palace of haunted dreams at the heart of the black lake. Tonight he seemed to hear only the thunderous silence, for somehow the music had lost him; or perhaps he had lost it, in that quiet moment inside his own heart of the night before; and the silence held no danger for him. This third night yet he was afraid again, for all his boldness; but it was not the cowering miserable fear of the first night, but the steady and knowledgeable fear of an old soldier who dares face an enemy too strong for him.

In his younger days the soldier had slipped into hostile camps when his colonel ordered him to, with but a few of his fellows, when the enemy was asleep or unguarded, to do what they could and then slip away again. It was because of one of these raids, not so successful as it might have been, that the soldier ever since was forewarned of a change in the weather by the slow pain in his right shoulder. He might be glad that the dagger had caught him in the shoulder and not in the leg, for he had still been able to run, trying by the pressure of his left hand to hold the blood from pumping out, the mist still rising inexorably before his eyes. He found himself with his legs braced and his hands clenched at his sides, staring at circling dancers, and that same mist before his eyes. He shook his head to clear it. He thought of scorning the fact that that particular memory chose to disturb him on this particular night; but he had not lived so long by ignoring such warnings as his instinct might give him. He was glad that this third night was to be his last; he felt as though the cloak of invisibility would not be a sufficient bar to all that he felt lurked here, beyond the lights, for very much longer. Some sort of dawn would come to betray him, shining through his shadow cloak, as a simpler sort of dawn had betrayed his nighttime stealth years ago.

And he listened again to what was not there behind the sorcerous music of this place, and thought that that dawn might be of his own making; there were some things that could not bear to be known, and he was walking too near to them.

He stood beside the great gates that led outside the castle to the night blackness beyond the ballroom light, and to the black water creeping around the docks. He saw the Princesses dancing in the graceful arms of their swains. The youngest danced past him, very near; so near he could see the transparent wisp of fair hair that had escaped the fine woven net and fallen across her eyes; and as she went past him he thought he saw her shudder, ever so slightly. Her eyes turned toward him, and he stopped breathing, thinking she might see some movement in the air. Her eyes searched the shadows where he stood wrapped in his cloak of shadows, as if she were certain that she would find something that she was looking for; and behind the fine veil of hair he saw fear sunk deep in her wide eyes. But her gaze passed over him and through him and back again without recognition; and then her tall partner whirled her into a figure of the dance that took her away from his dark corner, and he saw her no more.

He stayed where he was, thinking, watching; and he saw the eldest Princess walking again with her hand on the arm of her black captain; she passed through a high arch from the ballroom to the courtyard where he stood, a little way from him; and in her free hand she carried a jeweled goblet. The two of them paused just beyond the threshold, and the Princess glanced to one side. A low marble bench stood beside her. She lowered her hand with a swift gesture and left the cup upon it; and then walked away as her escort turned and led her, almost as if she wished him not to see what she had done. The soldier, without understanding what he did, went at once to that bench and lifted up the goblet. He peered inside, tilting it to the light so that he might see its bottom. It was empty. Some inlaid patterns glinted at him, but he could not see it clearly. He thought: "This will do also to show the King." And he hid the cup under his cloak.

That night too came to its end; and perhaps it was his own eagerness to be gone, but it seemed to him that the Princesses' step was slower tonight as they turned toward the boats, though from reluctance or weariness he could not say. But he walked so closely upon the youngest Princess's heels as she stepped into the last boat that nearly he trod upon her gown for a second time, and he caught himself back only just at the last.

As they disembarked on the far side of the lake the soldier stooped suddenly and dipped his goblet into the black water, raising it full to the brim; drops ran down its sides and across his hand like small crawling things with many legs, and his hand trembled, but he held the heavy cup grimly. He turned, the unpleasant touch of the black water still fresh on his skin, and watched the black hulls slide away like beetles across the lake's smooth surface. When he turned back again, the Princesses were already climbing the long stair, and he had to hurry to catch them up and lie back on his cot before they should look for him.

He was careful, for all his haste, that he spilled no further drop of the goblet's contents. He set it down beyond the head of his cot, and tossed his shadow cloak over it. When the eldest Princess came to look at him, he lay on his back, snorting a little in his sleep, as an old soldier who has drunk drugged wine might be expected to snort; but he watched her from under his lashes. She gave no sigh; and after a moment she went away.

He did not remember sleeping, that night. He heard the soft whisper of the elegant rainbow gowns being swept into chests and wardrobes; the heavy glassy clink of jewels into boxes; and a soft tired sound he thought might be of worn-out dancing slippers pushed gently under beds. Then there were the quiet subsiding sounds of mattresses and pillows, and the brittle swish of fresh sheets, the blowing out of candles and the sharp smell of the black wicks. And silence. The soldier lay on his back, his eyes wide open now in the darkness, and thought of all the things he had to think about, past and present; he dared not think of the future. But he put his memory in order as he was used to put his kit in order, with the brass and the buckles shining, the leather soaped and waxed, the tunic set perfectly.

He did not feel tired. And then at last some thin pale light came to touch his feet, and creep farther round the screen's edge to climb to his knees, and then leap over the screen's top to fall on his face. He watched the light, not liking it, for it should be the sweet wholesome light of dawn; but there was no window in the Long Gallery since the Princesses had slept here. And so he understood by its approach that the eldest Princess woke first, and lit her candle; and her first sister then awoke and lit hers; and so till the twelfth Princess felt the waxen light on her face and awoke in her turn, whose bed lay nearest the screen in the far corner.

The Princesses did not speak. Their morning toilette was completed quickly; and then there was a waiting sort of pause, and then he heard the sound of the King's key in the lock of the door to the Long Gallery that led into the castle, into the upper world. The door opened; and the sound of many skirts and petticoats told him the Princesses were leaving, although he heard no sound of footfall. Then the silence returned. The soldier sat up. His mind was alert, quiet but steady; but his body was stiff, especially the right shoulder.

He sat, waiting, wondering what would come to him. He creaked the mattress a little, wondering if they waited at the Gallery door already. They did. Two servants approached and set down a little table, and put a basin of water on it, and hung a towel over it. Then they folded the screen and set it to one side, and put the little table with the untouched lamp against the wall next to the screen. The soldier looked down the long row of twelve white beds, made up perfectly smooth so that one would think they never had been slept in; they might even have been carven from chalk or molded of the finest porcelain and polished with a silken cloth. He looked down and saw the tips of a pair of dancing shoes showing from beneath the bed nearest him. The fragile stuff they were made of sagged sadly down, and he did not need to see if there were holes in the bottoms.

He stood up, feeling as if his creaking bones might be heard by the waiting servants as the creaking mattress had been. He splashed his face with the water, then rubbed face and hands briskly with the towel. He pushed his shaggy hair back, knowing there was little else to be done with it. He looked up then, and the servants jerked their eyes away from the two heaps at the head of his cot and stared straight ahead of them. He wondered if these two men always waited on the third mornings of the Princesses' champions; and if so, what they had seen before.

He leaned down to pick up the heavy goblet; the cloak of shadows, nothing but a bit of black cloth to the eye, held round its stem, and clutched his wrist as if for reassurance. The wine-sodden cloak he left lying as it was.

He turned to the waiting servants, and they led the way to the door of the Long Gallery, down the stairs, and along the hall to the high chamber the soldier had sat in for three cheerless feasts at the King's right hand. Now the King sat in a tall chair at the end of this chamber; and his daughters stood on either hand. And around them, filling the hall till only a narrow way remained from the door to the feet of the King, were men and women who had heard of the new challenger come to try to learn how the Princesses danced holes in their shoes each night, locked in the Long Gallery by their father, who held the only key to that great mysterious door. And now they were come to hear what that hero had found.

The two servants that escorted him paused at the door to the great room, and made their bows; and the soldier went in alone. The subdued murmur of voices stopped at once upon his entrance. The hope and hopelessness that hung in the air were almost tangible; he could almost feel hands clutching at him, pleading with him. But he went on, much heartened; for the voices were real human voices, and he knew about hope and despair.

As he strode forward, one hand held to his breast with a thin shred of black dangling from the wrist and hand and what it held only a blur of shadows, someone stepped out of the crowd and stood before him. It was the captain of the guard, the man he called friend, however few the words they had actually exchanged; and in his hands he carried a bundle. This bundle he held out to the soldier, and the soldier took it; and he looked into his friend's eyes and smiled. The captain smiled back, anxiously, searching his face, and stepped back then; and the soldier went on to where the King sat. There he knelt, and on the first step of the dais he set two shrouded things from his two hands.

Then he stood, and looked at the King, who, sitting in the high throne, looked down at him.

"Well," said the King. He did not raise his voice, but
the King's voice was such of its own that it might reach
every corner with each word, as the King chose. This
"Well" now would ring in the ears of the man or woman
farthest from him in this crowded room. "You have spent
now three nights in the Long Gallery, guarding the sleep
of my daughters, while for three more nights they have
danced holes in their new shoes. Can you tell us how
it is that every night, although they may not stir from
their chamber, these new dancing slippers are worn quite
through, and each morning beneath each bed is not a pair
of shoes, but a few worn tatters of cloth?"

"Yes," said the soldier. "I can." His voice was no less
clear than the King's own; and a hush ran round the room
that was louder than words. "And I will." He bent and
picked up the bundle that the captain had given him; and
was surprised at the suppleness of his body, now that the
waiting was finished.

"At the foot of the eldest Princess's bed is a door of
stone that rises from the floor. Each night the Princesses
descend through that door, and down a long stairway
cut in the rock there. At first these stairs are dark, the
ceiling low and dank; but then the way opens on a cliff-
face that the stairs walk still down; and this open way
is lined to the cliff's foot with jeweled trees. On the first
night as I followed the Princesses I broke a branch of
one of these jeweled trees." And he opened the first
bundle and held the branch aloft, and the wicked gems
in the smooth white bole glittered and leaped like fire;
and a sigh wove through the crowd. The soldier had faced
the King as he spoke, although he fixed his eyes on the

King's hands as they lay serenely in his lap; now he saw them clench suddenly together and he raised his eyes to look at the King's face and saw there a sudden joy he could not quell for all his kingdom leap out of his eyes, not as a king but a father. The soldier noticed also that while the line of Princesses was now motionless, the hand of the youngest had risen and covered her face.

He drew his gaze back up the row to the eldest, but she stood quietly, her hands clasped before her and her eyes cast down.

"At the foot of the cliff," said the soldier, "there is a dark shore that edges a lake; and the waters of this lake are black, and—" there was a pause just long enough to be heard as a pause, and the soldier continued: "—and the waters of that lake do not sound as the waters of our lakes sound as they lap upon the shore."

He stooped and laid the jeweled branch on the second step of the dais, this but one step below the one on which the King's feet rested. It flickered at him as if its gems were winking eyes. As he straightened he found he had turned himself a little, facing more nearly toward where the eldest Princess stood than her father's throne; but he did not change his position again.

"At the edge of that lake are twelve boatmen, sculling their twelve lean black boats. The twelve captains wear black, and the oars are as black as the hulls. The twelve Princesses embark upon these boats, and are carried far —I know not how far, for what passes for sky in this underground place is dim and green, and soon darkens to the color of the lake itself as the boats pass over the water. Then a great palace looms up upon what is per-

haps an island, or perhaps a promontory of some dar
land on the far side of that lake; I only can tell you tha
the boats dock near the courtyard of this great palace
and the courtyard is ablaze with lights, as are the mag
nificent rooms within; but if one passes through thos
vast chambers to look upon the far side of the castle
for all the brilliance of the light, the shadows creep i
close, and are absolute no farther than a strong arm'
stone's throw from the palace gates. Nothing like moon o
star shines overhead.

"In these dazzling rooms your Princesses dance throug
the earth's night, partnered by the black ferrymen: bu
these have thrown off their black cloaks for the dancing
and are as dazzling in their beauty as the rooms tha
contain them—near as dazzling perhaps as the Princesse
themselves." The soldier spoke these words with no sens
of paying a compliment, but merely as a man speaks th
truth; and a few of the oldest members of the audienc
forgot for a moment the wonder of the story he told, an
looked at him sharply, and then smiled.

"There is a splendid throng in those great ballroom
one does not know where to look, and wherever one
eyes rest, the magnificence is bewildering, as is the grac
of the dancers. There is always music during those lon
hours that the Princesses dance their slippers to piece
the music reaches out to greet those who touch the pie
after the journey across the water; nearly it lifts one o
one's feet, whatever the will may say against it. But be
hind the music is silence, and something more tha
silence; something unnameable, and better so. And
heard no one of those dancers within those halls and tha

music ever address a word to another.

"Three nights I followed the Princesses to this place, walking down the stairs behind them, standing in the bottom of the twelfth black boat with a Princess before me and a captain behind; three nights I followed them again back to the castle of their father, and ran ahead of them at the last, to be lying snoring on my bed when they returned." But he spoke no word, yet, of how this was accomplished without any knowing.

"On the third night at the palace I brought something away with me." He bent again, and picked up the shapeless blur of shadows. He peeled the whispering rag away, and let it fall to his feet, where it lay motionless; but he was not unaware of its touch, and he wondered at its uncommon stillness. He held the goblet up as he held the branch, and those whose eyes followed it in the first moments thought it was as if the unshielded sun shone in the room, and before their eyes colors shifted and swam, and they could not see their neighbors, but seemed for that moment to be in a castle beyond imagining grander than their King's proud castle, surrounded by a crowd of people unnaturally, beautiful.

But the vision cleared and the soldier spoke again, and those who had seen something they had not understood in the sudden brilliance of the thing he had held up to them listened uneasily, but knowing that what he said was true. "This goblet is from the shadow-held palace underground, where the Princesses dance holes in their shoes." He lowered the goblet, and looked into it. The black water shifted as his hand trembled, and the surface glittered like the facets of polished stone. The noise

of the water as it touched the sides was like the distant
cries of the imprisoned. "In it I dipped up some of the
water of that lake I crossed six times."

As he said this, the cries seemed suddenly to have
words in them, as once he had heard the water talking
secrets to the shore; but this time, in earth's broad day-
light, he was horribly afraid of the words he might hear
that they might somehow harm his world, taint the sky
and the sunlight. And he held the cup abruptly away
from him, as far as his arm would reach. The water rose
up to the brim and spilled over, with a nasty thin shriek
like victory; and it fell to the floor with a hiss. Where it
fell there rose a shadow, and the shadow seemed dread-
fully to take shape; and the people who stood watching
moaned. The soldier stood stricken with the knowledge
of what he had done; the King made no sign.

The shadow moved; it ebbed and rose again, bulking
larger in the light; and a leg of it, if it was a leg, thrust
back, feeling its way. It touched the discarded cloak
crouched at the soldier's feet.

And the shadow was gone as if it had never been. Most
of those who had seen it were never sure of what they
saw; some, who knew about the nightmares where an
unseen Thing pursues without reason or mercy, believed
in this waking Thing more easily; but in later years remembered only that once they had had a nightmare more
terrible than the rest, and there was no memory of what
had happened the day that the twelve dancing Princesses'
enchantment was broken. But about the soldier's tale all
remembered his description of the underground land the
Princesses had been bound to for so many nights with a

deep-felt fear that could not entirely be accounted for in the words the soldier used.

But then too there was little time for thought, for what was certain was that the ground underfoot suddenly rose up to strike at those who had so long taken its imperturbability for granted. It rose up, and sank away again, and quivered alarmingly, and several people cried out, though none was hurt; a few stumbled and fell to their knees. A dull but thunderous roar was heard at some distance they could not guess at. A servant came in during the stunned silence following the half-believed shadow and the unknown roar, and explained, so far as he could; and bowed shakily, and went away again. The floor of the walled-in Long Gallery had collapsed, burying forever the entrance to the underground lake.

No one knew what the Princesses thought, and no one inquired. When any dared stop feeling themselves to be sure they were there, and not home in bed, and looking surreptitiously at those who stood around them, who were looking surreptitiously back, and free to raise their eyes and look at the royal daughters again, the Princesses' faces were calm, their eyes downcast, as before. But those who stood nearest the soldier and the King and the twelve Princesses thought that the King and his daughters were whiter than they were wont to be. And yet at the same time there was something like the joy the soldier had seen pulling at the King's face pulling as well at his daughters' eyes and mouths and hands.

The soldier knew what had happened, and believed; he knew about nightmares. But he knew also that there were nightmares that happened when one was awake,

which was a knowledge denied most of the quiet farm
folk and city merchants present around him. And he was
appalled at this shadow he had freed. He looked down
at his feet. A wisp of black, gossamer thin, delicate as a
lady's veil, lay before him. He knelt to pick it up, and
it stirred gently against his palm; and he heard as he knelt
the King's voice speaking to him.

"Can you tell us how you succeeded in this thing?
How none tried to prevent you from going where you
would?"

The soldier straightened up once more, holding the
terrible goblet, empty now, chaste and still, in one hand,
and the little bit of black in the other. "An old woman
gave me a cloak," he said slowly. "A black cloak, to make
me invisible; for I told her where I was bound, and why;
and though I had done her but a small service that any
might have done in my place, she wished to give me this
gift." He looked up, met the King's eyes. "And she
warned me not to drink the wine the Princesses would
offer me when I lay down in my corner of the Long
Gallery; and warned me too that not to drink might be
more difficult than it seems to tell it."

"This cloak," said the King. "Where is it now?"

"I do not know," said the soldier, and the hand not
holding the cup closed gently around the shred of black
rag that was a cloak no longer.

The King stood up from his throne then and stepped
down till he stood on the floor next to the soldier; and
in his eyes was the gladness the soldier had seen flare up
when first he began his story; but there was no attempt
to moderate or conceal it now, and it struck the soldier

full in the face. And something like that joy—for a poor and weary soldier has little knowledge of joy—rose up in the soldier's heart. And he thought as he had thought three nights before: "This is the commander that I fought for, although I did not know it; I am glad that I have been permitted to meet him." But as he looked upon the King's face now, he thought that the drinking of their sovereign's health was not a wasted tradition at all. Years fell away from the soldier as he stood smiling at his commander, and certain memories he had never been able to shut out of his dreams went quietly to sleep themselves. The goblet dropped from his hand without his knowing. It fell to the floor with a dull and heavy clang; and not one eye followed it, for all were looking at the King and the man who had returned him his happiness. The goblet was forgotten; and much later, the servants who came to set the room to rights did not find it, although several of them knew it should be there to be found.

Then the King said so that all the people might hear: "You know the reward for the breaking of this spell: you shall marry one of my daughters, and she shall be Queen and you King after me, and the eldest of your children shall sit on the throne after you."

The soldier found that he was looking over the King's shoulder, and his eyes, without his asking them to, found the down-turned face of the eldest Princess. As her father finished speaking she looked up, and met the soldier's gaze; and then he knew that the odd stirring beneath his breast bone that he had felt in the face of the King's happiness was joy indeed, for it welled up so strongly it could not be mistaken.

"Give me the eldest," he heard his voice say, "for I am no longer young."

And the eldest Princess stepped forward before her father had the chance to say yea or nay, and walked to him, and held out her hand to him; but he did not realize till her fingers closed around his that he had reached out his hand to her.

The people cheered; the soldier heard it, but did not notice when it first began. The Princess's eyes, that looked into his now so clearly and peacefully, were an unusual color, a sweet lavender that was almost blue; and in them he read a wisdom that comforted him, for it held a sense of youth that had nothing to do with years.

He did not know what it was the Princess saw as she looked at him that made her smile so wonderfully; but he thought he might learn, and so he smiled back.

EPILOGUE

THE WEDDING was celebrated but a fortnight later; time enough only to invite everyone, not only those who lived in the city or nearby, but those who lived far up in the mountains, those even who lived beyond the kingdom's borders who would reach out to grasp the hand of friendship thus offered, and come and dance at the wedding. There was barely time enough for all the barrels of wine and of flour and sugar, and haunches of beef and venison, and all the fruits that the city and the ships at its docks might furnish, to be brought to the castle and dealt with magnificently by the royal cooks. And all the time that the cooks were baking and stewing and roasting and arranging, all the seamstresses and tailors were sewing new gowns and tunics, and the jesters studied new tricks, and the theatrical troupes went over new sketches, and the musicians unearthed all the dancing music they had once played with such delight, and learned it all over again, but even better than before. It was the grandest wedding that all the people in a country all working together might bring about; and there was help from neighboring countries and their kings too, whether they could attend or not, for many were glad to see their old friend restored to happiness. And there were a number of noble sons thoughtfully dispatched to look over the eleven other Princesses. And the gaiety was such that people felt quite free to compliment all the Princesses on how beautifully they danced; and if perhaps the eldest danced the best of all, seven of her sisters were nonetheless betrothed by the end of the week's celebration, and the other four by the time she and her new husband returned from their bridal trip.

The youngest Princess married the captain of the guard. Once this might have been thought too lowly a match for a royal Princess; but her fiancé had been seen to be the right-hand man of the new Crown Prince.

And an ostler who had once told a restless soldier the story of the twelve dancing Princesses came to the wedding by special invitation, which included a horse from the royal stables to ride on; and this ostler later admired all the King's stable and stud so intelligently that room was found for him there. And by the time he had taught thirty-two young Princes and forty-seven young Princesses how to ride and drive and take proper care of their horses, he was Master of the Stable and ready to retire.

On their bridal trip the Crown Prince and his Princess rode up the road that had first brought the Prince to the city; and the Prince recognized much of what he had seen on his journey. But they found no small cottage near a well where such should be, nor any old woman like the one he still remembered. They went so far as to ask some of the folk who lived along the road to the King's city if they knew of her; but none did.

About the Author . . .

Jennifer Carolyn Robin McKinley was born in her mother's home town of Warren, Ohio, and grew up in various places all over the world because her father was in the Navy. She read Andrew Lang's *Blue Fairy Book* for the first time in California; *The Chronicles of Naria* for the first time in New York; *The Lord of the Rings* for the first time in Japan; *The Once and Future King* for the first time in Maine. She is still inclined to keep track of her life by recalling what books she was reading at a given time. Other than books she counts as her major preoccupations grand opera and long walks, both of which she claims keep the blood flowing and the imagination limber. At present she divides her time between Maine and New York City.

Her first novel, *Beauty: A Retelling of the Story of Beauty and the Beast,* was published in the fall of '78. *The Door in the Hedge* is her second book. Her third, *The Blue Sword*— the first book of a trilogy—was published in the fall of '82; the second book of the trilogy, *The Hero and the Crown,* was published in the fall of '84.

MAGICQUEST ™

A new fantasy series featuring the best in Young Adult Fantasy— classic titles of magic and adventure by the top authors in the fantasy field, in paperback for the very first time!

THE THROME OF THE ERRIL OF SHERILL #1
Patricia A. McKillip _____ 80839-5/$2.25
THE PERILOUS GARD #2
Elizabeth Marie Pope _____ 65956-X/$2.25
THE SEVENTH SWAN #3
Nicholas Stuart Gray _____ 75955-6/$2.25
THE ASH STAFF #4 Paul R. Fisher _____ 03115-3/$2.25
TULKU #5 Peter Dickinson _____ 82630-X/$2.25
THE DRAGON HOARD #6
Tanith Lee _____ 16621-0/$2.25
THE HAWKS OF FELLHEATH #7
Paul R. Fisher _____ 31906-8/$2.25
THE MAGIC THREE OF SOLATIA #8
Jane Yolen _____ 51562-2/$2.25
POWER OF THREE #9
Diana Wynne Jones _____ 67630-8/$2.25
THE PRINCESS AND THE THORN #10
Paul R. Fisher _____ 67918-8/$2.25
TIME PIPER #11 Delia Huddy _____ 81205-8/$2.25
THE MAGICIANS OF CAPRONA #12
Diana Wynne Jones _____ 51556-8/$2.25
Prices may be slightly higher in Canada.